"LUKE, IT WAS JUST ONE NIGHT, THAT'S ALL," Alex insisted.

"It was more," he said.

"No."

"It could be more still."

"No." She shook her head. "I can't. Don't you get it, you're a—"

He pulled her even closer. "A suspect. And that makes me off-limits. That makes it easier for you. You don't want to believe I'm innocent, do you? Because you'd have to deal with me on an emotional level."

She couldn't let him know what he did to her, how he made her feel.

"You know what's really getting to you?" He released her hand and touched her cheek. "I know your weakness, that you're not all badass investigator." His hand slid to her neck, caressing it. His voice pinned her, mesmerized her, sent tingles of sensation along her spine. "I've seen the woman beneath—the one who feels passion, the one who feels pain. And you can't stand it. You're not upset because you think I'm guilty. You're mad as hell because you know I'm innocent. . . ."

Loveswept® 898

JUST ONE NIGHT

EVE GADDY

BANTAM BOOKS
NEW YORK · TORONTO · LONDON · SYDNEY · AUCKLAND

JUST ONE NIGHT

A Bantam Book / August 1998

ISBN 0-553-44631-2

Published simultaneously in the United States and Canada

*Bantam Books are published by Bantam Books, a division of Bantam Dou-
bleday Dell Publishing Group, Inc. Its trademark, consisting of the words
"Bantam Books" and the portrayal of a rooster, is Registered in U.S.
Patent and Trademark Office and in other countries. Marca Registrada.
Bantam Books, 1540 Broadway, New York, New York 10036.*

PRINTED IN THE UNITED STATES OF AMERICA

OPM   10 9 8 7 6 5 4 3 2 1

With thanks to Elizabeth Diaz for answering my questions about the Dallas Bomb Unit. Also many thanks to Becky Swearingen and Bill Supan for their help with my questions about construction and architecture.

ONE

No one had told Alex Sheridan her trip to San Diego would be free. Giving a lecture on bomb awareness to a group of architects seemed a small price to pay—except she'd forgotten that public speaking made her want to chug antacid in massive quantities.

The Hotel Del Coronado, a gorgeous example of Victorian architectural splendor, boasted opulent conference rooms encircling a courtyard filled with wine-colored bougainvillea, fan and date palms, and massed flowers of every conceivable color and variety. A great place to give a lecture if it weren't so distracting, Alex thought, glancing out the window before she looked back at her notes. She was at the tail end of her speech and she could almost smell the sea breeze calling her to the beach.

The pest in the front row raised his hand

for the twelfth time since she had begun the lecture. Wearily, she nodded at him.

"Detective Sheridan, have you ever been personally involved in a case that used a car as a vehicle for a bomb?"

At the unexpected question, memories exploded in Alex's mind. The conference room seemed to fade, the people disappearing, as she was catapulted back into the past. . . .

Alex stared at the charred car parked outside the elementary-school administration building and sucked in a deep breath. Why hadn't the car exploded when the fire started? She'd find out soon enough. Focus, she told herself, knowing she'd be starting the long walk any second now.

"Heads, it's mine," Jenna said, interrupting her mental preparations.

Alex frowned at her partner, watching her toss blonde hair back from her face. "It's a bomb, Jenna, not a game. Maybe a hang fire, maybe a booby trap. And you're not ready." But seeing the enthusiasm sparkling in Jenna's green eyes, Alex knew it would be impossible to convince the young woman of that.

And on the face of it, her partner was ready. Jenna had been through the training, put in her time. She should be ready. Only Alex didn't believe it. There was more to it than being

technically prepared. You had to be emotion-
ally ready as well. To Jenna everything was part
of some grand game, one she was always sure
she'd win.

Unsurprisingly, Jenna ignored her, flipping
the quarter easily despite her bulky bomb suit.
She looked down at the ground, then back at
Alex with a cheeky grin. "Heads it is. You lose.
See you in a few." She put on her helmet, then
flipped Alex a two-fingered salute before she
turned and walked toward the vehicle as briskly
as her body armor and sixty pounds of gear
allowed.

Alex shook her head, trying to decide if she
was simply being overprotective or if she had a
good reason for denying her partner this "bap-
tism by fire." If she was going to be a full
member of the bomb unit, Jenna would have to
take the same risks everyone else did. She was
just so damned young, Alex thought, even
though she herself was only a few years older
than Jenna. Had she ever been that young?
That arrogant?

Jenna approached the vehicle slowly, care-
fully examining the surrounding area before lying on the ground to inspect the undercarriage
with mirrors. After what seemed to Alex like
hours, she rose and glanced back at the group
of her colleagues, waiting a considerable distance away. She made no sign, indicating she
hadn't seen anything suspicious yet.

Watching Jenna inspect the interior of the car without touching anything, Alex tried to still her pounding nerves, licking her lips to camouflage a mouth gone dry with tension. As Jenna rounded the right rear bumper she stretched out her hand to open the car door. The right rear door, just as they'd all been taught. The door least likely to initiate a bomb.

Except . . .

Experience and gut instinct pierced Alex with a sharp sense of doom. *"No! Jenna, no!"* The words ripped out of her throat at the same time as the bomb exploded, a torrent of red, yellow, and orange flames erupting from the vehicle, black smoke billowing outward in malicious plumes of destruction, metal flying in deadly arcs.

Her senses shot into overload. The stench of burning rubber, and worse, imprinted in her nostrils. The wholesale annihilation of everything within a hundred-foot radius of the blast burned its way into her mind with the same abandon as the scorching flames leaping from the wrecked vehicle. The wail of sirens, shrill screams from the bystanders, cursing and orders from the rest of the unit jumbled together in an awful cacophony of devastation.

"Detective Sheridan?"

A man's voice repeated her name, jerking Alex back to the present as quickly as she'd been tossed into the past. She blinked and stared at him. "I'm sorry . . . I—" Unnerved, she shook her head and drew in a breath while her tormentor plowed on.

"I asked if you had ever been involved in a case that used a car as—"

"Let's get back to the topic at hand," she interrupted, pulling herself together and giving the questioner the haughtiest, frostiest glare she could manage. "Bomb awareness, particularly as it pertains to security in buildings under construction."

Somehow, she finished the lecture, thankful she'd been nearing the end before the question had thrown her into a tumult. She had thought three years would be enough distance not to have that particular piece of her past revived. She'd been wrong.

Jenna, she thought, the pain, as always, settling around her heart in an icy casing. Smart. Cocky. Irreverent.

Dead.

Sometime later, alone and nursing a drink in the darkly intimate lobby bar of the Hotel Del Coronado, Alex tried to decide why a simple question had disturbed her so. She'd given lectures before, been asked similar questions before, and never reacted so strongly. It wasn't as if she never thought about the past, never thought about her partner's death. She'd been over it a thousand times and more, until finally, she'd dealt with the trauma and gone on with her life.

Or thought she had.

Maybe it had shaken her so much because that particular bombing—the worst of her career—had taken place three years ago this week. The question during her lecture that afternoon had brought it all back. Pain, anger, regret. Guilt.

Would Jenna's death always haunt her? The case was closed, the culprit brought to justice. Jenna was dead and nothing would ever bring her back. Why, Alex wondered, couldn't she find peace with what had happened?

Closing her eyes, she rubbed at her temples, attempting to push back the grim memories of the past. She didn't want to think about Jenna. Didn't want to think about work. Didn't want to think, period.

"I enjoyed your lecture this afternoon," a deep male voice said.

Alex glanced up at the man standing beside her table. Even with the dim lighting obscuring his face, a jolt of recognition, of intense feminine awareness, shot through her. She'd noticed him the first day of the conference—and every day since. And the more she saw of him, the more she found herself fascinated by him.

Why, she couldn't say. Something about him spoke to her of danger. Excitement. The last things a bomb-unit investigator needed. She got plenty of both on the job.

Lord, he was tall, she thought, forced to tilt her head back to look at him. And as broad-shouldered as a football player. He wore a short-sleeved dusty blue knit shirt that stretched enticingly across a wide chest, and tan cotton slacks that looked expensive yet comfortable.

Black hair, worn a little too long to be conservative, brushed his collar. Piercing gray eyes dominated a rugged face with a straight, strong nose. Whoa, she thought. Better watch out or she'd start salivating.

"Can I buy you a drink?" he asked when she didn't reply, gesturing at her nearly empty glass.

Despite the attraction, or perhaps because of it, the word *no* rose automatically to her lips. His smile, along with the wicked gleam in his eyes, issued a challenge, as if he knew what she was thinking and dared her to do the unexpected. And why not? she suddenly thought. What was the big deal in having a drink with a man in a public place? Anything would be better than dealing with the memories plaguing her now.

He took the chair she nodded at, snaring the waitress immediately with a hand signal. Alex eyed him with grudging respect. She'd been trying to catch the waitress's eye for the last ten minutes with a distinct lack of success.

"Margarita. Rocks, with lots of salt," she told the waitress.

Dark eyebrows rose above the man's eyes. "Two," he said, and turned back to Alex. "Are you celebrating or forgetting?"

"Who says it has to be either?" she asked, taken aback by his perceptiveness. Or maybe it was a lucky guess.

A smile tilted his mouth. "Isn't it? I'd say"—he paused and looked her over, sending a tingle of awareness to the pit of her stomach—"forgetting." His voice held a hint of gravel and steel that made the blood throb in her veins.

He gave an impression of strength and virility, exuding an almost animal magnetism she wasn't accustomed to dealing with. Not what she'd have expected in an architect. He seemed the type of man to have a more physical profession, rather than the thoughtful one she imagined architecture to be.

The waitress returned with their drinks. Alex took a fortifying sip before answering him. "Forgetting," she said at last, wondering why she'd told him the truth. "How did you know?"

He tapped her glass. "Tip-off number one. A beautiful woman drinking tequila alone."

Alex had been called beautiful before. She

attributed it mostly to her hair. A lot of men seemed fascinated by red hair, especially when it was worn long, like hers. But the way he said it, in that deep bass voice, did strange things to her insides. Still, she wasn't about to let him know that.

"Besides," he added, swallowing some of his own drink, "I heard your lecture today."

"So you said." She tilted her head, considering him. "It was that obvious?"

Muscles rippled across his chest and arms when he shrugged, noticeable even beneath the material of his shirt. "To me it was. I don't know about anyone else. I've seen that look before."

"What look?"

For a moment he didn't speak, seeming to consider her question. "A kind of blankness that means you're not there," he said at length. "You've gone someplace else, someplace you don't want to be."

"Like the expression in your eyes right now?" she asked quietly.

He remained silent, contemplating her, but somehow she knew she'd been right. Uneasy from his steady regard, she dropped her gaze to the table. His hand caressed his glass and she fought a sudden image of what those long, tanned fingers would look like against pale skin. Her skin. Good Lord, what was the matter with her? She didn't even know his name.

Raising her gaze to his face again didn't help. Staring at his mouth brought on even more inappropriate visions. "You have the advantage of me." He lifted an eyebrow, and she continued. "You know who I am, but I don't know who you are."

"Luke Morgan," he said, extending a hand.

A little hesitantly, she placed her hand in his. "Alex Sheridan." Touching him had been a mistake, she realized. His clasp was firm, his palm dry, and for reasons she couldn't fathom, a swell of sensation zinged up her arm. Maybe she didn't need any more tequila.

"So, you're an architect." *Oh, that's witty, Alex.*

A smile tugged at one corner of his mouth as he nodded. "And you're an investigator with the Dallas Bomb Unit."

She frowned. "I've got an idea. Why don't we not talk about work."

"Fine with me. Shall we talk about forgetting? And ways to accomplish it?"

"Such as?" she asked, curious to hear his answer.

"A walk in the moonlight. A dance on the terrace." His smile broadened. "Sex on the beach. Ever had it?"

Barely restraining her jaw from dropping, Alex stared at him. If she had any sense she'd slap him, or at the least tell him to leave. But he was smiling at her as if sharing a joke.

"It's a drink," he said, nodding toward the bar. "What did you think I meant?"

Alex started laughing. She couldn't help it. "I'm sure you know exactly what I thought."

"You have to admit, it's an icebreaker."

"You're lucky it hasn't gotten your jaw broken."

"I like to live dangerously," he murmured, his eyes glinting with devilment.

The waitress miraculously reappeared, allowing Alex a chance to collect her thoughts. A good thing too, she thought. It had been a long time since a man had pursued her so blatantly. She liked it, even if she wasn't sure what she wanted to do about it. Feeling reckless, she didn't protest when he ordered another round.

"You're direct, aren't you?" she said.

"When the situation calls for it."

Okay, she could be direct too. "Are you married?"

"No." He let that hang for a moment, then added, "Does it matter?"

Only if she decided . . . No, she wasn't quite that reckless. Was she? "I don't know. I have a feeling it might."

She thought he'd jump on that comment, but he only said, "Have a lot of married men hit on you?"

"Some. Is that what you're doing? Hitting on me?"

"I'm not married, remember? And I prefer to think of it as appreciating beauty."

She laughed, the admiring gleam in his eyes giving her a rush of pleasure. "That certainly sounds better."

"Maybe because it's true."

She arched an eyebrow in challenge. "Most women like to at least pretend that a man is interested in something besides her looks."

"I haven't talked to you enough to know much more about you." His fingers feathered a touch on the back of her hand as their gazes met. "But I'd like to. Very much."

Alex let out a breath she hadn't realized she'd been holding. Oh, he was good. Dangerously so.

So they talked. About art and music. About books, movies, and sports. They discussed everything, except, thank God, her work, as if they'd known each other for months instead of minutes. Strange, she thought, how easily he drew her out when she wasn't ordinarily a chatty person. Usually, she was the expert on getting information from people.

Much later, she noticed they'd both finished their drinks. He must have realized it too. Instead of ordering another, he stood and held out his hand to her.

"Let's take a walk. The smoke is getting to me."

She'd attributed the haze to tequila and was

pleasantly surprised to realize he was right. "Where to?" she asked, suddenly wary. His room, she bet, wishing he wouldn't say it.

He smiled wickedly, like he knew what she was thinking. "The beach. Have you been out there at night?"

Along with relief came a swift stab of disappointment. She told herself she was crazy even to consider . . . what she was considering. Her cautious side knew what she should do. The side that sought oblivion from the past wasn't so sure.

"I went out there last night," she said. "I love the beach at night. During the day, too, but"—she grimaced at the fair skin of her arms, revealed by her short-sleeved forest-green suit jacket—"I've got the redhead's curse. I don't tan, I burn."

She allowed him to help her to her feet, realizing when she stood beside him just how big he was. Though at five-foot-nine she'd never considered herself a small woman, she felt positively tiny next to Luke Morgan.

Tracing his fingers along her forearm, he looked into her eyes and said, "It would be a crime to burn skin like yours."

Her heart rate jumped in anticipation. No use denying the attraction. Every time he touched her, casually or not so casually, as he was doing now, sexual tension arced between them. Still, that didn't mean she had to do anything about it. He'd only asked for a moonlight stroll.

If she was going to walk on the beach, Alex decided, she'd do it right. Heels and panty hose didn't mix with sand. Excusing herself, she went in search of the ladies' room.

Luke had been half-afraid he'd seen the last of her when she disappeared. Normally, he'd have shrugged it off, but Alex Sheridan wasn't the type of woman he usually took up with. For one thing, she was far too classy. Sexy. A subtle sexy instead of in-your-face. In fact, she was a knockout. And she sure as hell didn't look, or dress, like any cop he'd ever known.

She returned with a smile on her face, her purse in one hand, her shoes dangling from the other. His gaze dropped to dynamite legs beneath a short dark green skirt. Bare legs. God have mercy, he thought, wondering what those creamy-skinned legs would feel like beneath his palms and hoping he'd get the chance to find out.

He'd been wrong. She was definitely his type.

When they reached the beach, she halted. "You're not going to walk in the sand wearing shoes?"

Luke heard the laughter underlying her words and smiled. "That would be pointless, wouldn't it?" He took off his shoes and socks, carrying them as they walked down to the waterline, just out of reach of the tide. Once there, he dropped them in the sand, then took her shoes and dropped them beside his. "I don't think anyone will bother a couple of pairs of shoes." And he had other things he'd rather hold than shoes. Like a redhead named Alex. For now, though, he contented himself with holding her hand. He was a patient man when necessary.

For the first time in months—hell, make that years—he was enjoying talking to a woman. He wasn't big on conversation anyway, and when he was with a woman, talk was usually the last thing on his mind. But Alex interested him. He must be losing it, he decided. Here he was, on a deserted beach at night with a gorgeous redhead and he was thinking about her mind?

They walked in companionable silence for a while before she spoke. "Earlier you said you'd seen the look before. When I was speaking and . . ." Her voice trailed off.

It hadn't been difficult to recognize, he thought. Her eyes had gone from blank to anguished. She had turned inward, seeing some gut-wrenching event in her past. He'd done it too many times himself not to know what was happening to her.

"You covered it up well, but I've been there

myself." Understatement. His time with the navy SEALs had given him nightmares for years afterward. Thank God he'd finally quit having them.

"I thought that's what you meant." She stopped and looked up at him. "So tell me, Luke, what do you do to forget?"

The smell of salt water tinged the night breeze, taunting his senses with memories. He smiled down at her, wondering what she'd do if he told her his preferred cure. Instead he said, "Drinking works. Sometimes. Except it gives you a hangover which can be nearly as bad as the memories. And after a while it quits working."

"It's been three years," she said, almost wistfully. "I thought I'd gotten past it."

"Some things never go away. They fade, but they're always there." Luke could still remember the sick feeling he'd had when he found out the truth about his old man. And that had been over twenty years ago.

Alex was staring, not at him but out to sea. At some window to the past, he suspected. Cupping her face in his hands, he brought her startled gaze to meet his. "But the best way I've found"—he rubbed his thumb over her soft, tempting lips—"is this." Slowly, he lowered his mouth to hers, waiting for her to pull back. When she didn't, he captured her mouth, tracing her lips with the tip of his tongue until she opened and invited him inside.

He sank his hands into her hair, wanting to know what she looked like wearing nothing but that thick, rich mass flowing over her like a flame. Luke had kissed a lot of women in the past and enjoyed them all, but Alex was the stuff dreams were made of. His tongue swept her mouth thoroughly, enticing hers until she began making teasing forays of her own.

Her purse dropped to the sand beside them, then her arms encircled his neck, her body pressing close to his. Their tongues touched, retreated, touched again in a potent, sexy-as-hell rhythm. She moaned throatily as his arms tightened around her, as the kiss deepened and desire flashed hot between them. He knew for a fact that if he didn't stop soon, sex on the beach wouldn't be just a drink.

When Alex Sheridan kissed a man, he thought, she didn't do it halfway.

Still holding her in his arms, Luke drew back and smiled at her. Her eyes had gone dreamy. "So, Alex, what do you think?"

"I think I'll have to reserve judgment."

"Until?"

"Until you kiss me again."

TWO

With a muttered curse, Luke shoved his chair back from his desk and rose to pace the length of his office. Frustrated by his recent lack of productivity, he slapped his pen against his hand in disgust. Red ink squirted out, staining his palm. Red, dammit, he thought. It would be.

In the three weeks that had passed since his return from San Diego, he had thought about Alex Sheridan every day. It was driving him crazy. Why would a one-night fling with a woman, however beautiful and sexy he had found her, stay with him like it had?

He had a feeling he knew. She'd touched something in him besides his libido. His . . . sense of compassion? That was an emotion he thought he'd lost long ago. But when he'd seen her face for that brief, unguarded moment during her lecture, he'd wanted to help her. He'd thought his days as a white knight long over, the desire killed by his disillusionment with his naval career, but her vulnerability had gotten to him. He'd bet she was ordinarily very good at covering that vulnerability. And that was probably why she'd hightailed it out of his room the next morning before he awakened.

He should have expected her to leave. Should have been relieved that she had. No messy morning-after scene when they avoided each other's eyes and both said things they didn't mean. But he hadn't been relieved. He'd been angry.

From her bio in the conference brochure, Luke knew Alex lived in Dallas, or at least in the surrounding area. He hadn't told her he did too. And she hadn't asked. The lady hadn't been looking for commitment, she'd been looking to forget.

God knew he wasn't a man to tie himself up with a woman. But it rankled that she'd been able to forget him, apparently, when he couldn't forget her. Given her profession, he knew she'd be able to track him down. If she wanted to.

Luke wasn't sure what he thought about that night with Alex. About making love with Alex. Obviously, it had been about sex—lust and physical attraction, especially the first time. But even that first time he'd felt something more than sex between them. And the second time . . .

He'd awakened in the predawn hours to find her in the grips of a nightmare. After he'd awakened her, he offered to talk about it. She refused, and instead they'd made love again. And like the first time, it had been fantastic, and yet they had related on a level deeper than the physical. An emotional level, he supposed, frowning. Why it had happened with Alex when he hadn't connected, really connected, with any woman in the preceding thirty-six years of his life, he couldn't say. It made no sense to him.

Luke liked to keep his private life simple. Unentangled. So why couldn't he accept that her leaving the next morning was the best thing that could have happened to him? Especially given his reaction to her. She must have felt it too. Maybe that was why she had left.

Oh, hell, what difference did it make? he asked himself. Alex Sheridan would bore him in time, or demand more than he had to give, just like every other woman he'd known.

But he was tempted, extremely tempted, to try to see her again. If only to prove to himself that night had been a fluke and all his imaginings of some deeper connection had been just that. Imagination.

His secretary came in just then with the blueprints for the Alsobrook project. Kathy was in her mid-fifties, practical and unflappable, with improbably dyed bright orange hair that seemed at odds with her no-nonsense manner. Since she was the best secretary Luke had ever had, he didn't give a flip if she came to work sporting a purple Mohawk and a nose ring.

"You've got an appointment at the site at five-thirty with Waylon Black," she reminded him as she laid the rolled-up paper on his desk. "That's fifteen minutes from now."

"Damn," he said, glancing at his watch to discover she was right. He had too much to do to waste time thinking about a woman. Even a woman like Alex Sheridan.

On his way to the site, he considered the Alsobrook building. He'd busted his butt for months to secure the contract for the project, and it was turning out to be everything he'd hoped for. With any luck, and a lot of hard work, it should pull his career out of the nose-dive it had suffered in the last couple of years.

He found his general contractor in the temporary building set up as his on-site office. As usual, Waylon had his feet propped on the desk, a phone receiver to one ear and a cup of coffee—probably his thirtieth of the day—in hand. "Right, tomorrow," he was saying. "And if you don't deliver tomorrow, then you can kiss the contract good-bye."

Swearing without heat, he slammed down

the receiver and grinned at Luke. His short brown hair stuck straight up, testimony to his habit of raking his hands through it when something frustrated him. "You know the old saying, give 'em an inch . . ."

"Problems?" Luke asked, his hands in his pockets as he rocked back on his heels.

"Nah. Nothing I can't handle." Swinging his legs down, Waylon added, "He just needs to know he can't jerk us around on delivery times. Coffee?"

Luke held up a hand. "No, thanks." Besides being addicted to caffeine, Waylon was notoriously unpicky about what his coffee tasted like. Fresh, burned, weak, strong, as long as it had caffeine in it, Waylon didn't care.

"Glad you're here, Luke." He hitched his jeans up in a vain attempt to hide the spare tire around his middle. "I've got some things to show you that you'll want to check out. But I've got to tell you, things are going so smoothly here, it's damn near spooky."

"About time, don't you think?"

"Damn straight," Waylon said.

Their gazes met, and Luke knew they were each remembering the last two years and the struggle it had been to keep afloat, much less prosper.

Waylon Black was one of the few men Luke trusted. As much as he was capable of trusting anyone, which at this point wasn't a lot. Still,

Luke reminded himself that the contractor had proved himself loyal.

And not many contractors had been willing to take a chance on Luke Morgan after the debacle, courtesy of James Bennett, involving Morgan & Bennett Architectural Associates. Even changing the name of his company to 2000 A.D.—Architectural Designs for Tomorrow—hadn't done much good. Too many people knew Luke owned it. Guilt by association was a powerful force, particularly in the business world.

A good thing James was dead, Luke thought, or he would have been tempted to kill him himself.

As Luke toured the partially completed building with Waylon, he saw the finished product in his mind. He wanted to create an impression of glass and air, and he believed he could do it. The conference in San Diego had been surprisingly useful. Luke had returned with some great ideas for final touches to this project as well as plans for new ones.

The structure before him was as good, maybe even better, than anything he'd yet created. A true design for the future. Furthermore, he had every hope that it would come in on budget, especially with Waylon Black in charge. Waylon could cut more corners than anyone Luke knew without compromising quality. Functional as well as beautiful, the Al-

sobrook Investments Building would fit per-
fectly with the sleek, mirrored skyscrapers
gleaming on the Dallas horizon.

"It's good, Luke," Waylon said, picking up
on his thoughts, as he had a knack for doing.
"The best work you've done yet."

Luke couldn't help smiling. It was gratify-
ing to know that someone whose opinion he
respected agreed with him.

After surveying the construction site, dealing with a few glitches, discussing potential
problems, and setting up a time for another
meeting the following week, Luke and Waylon
walked to their cars.

"Ready to get rid of that 'Vette yet?"
Waylon asked.

Grinning, Luke shook his head. "In your
dreams, Black. But you'll be the first to know if
I change my mind." The chances of Luke's
selling the classic '66 white Corvette he'd
bought as a junker and lovingly restored were
between slim and none, and Waylon knew it.
They still played out this scene every time the
contractor caught sight of it.

Parked beside Waylon's rusted black
pickup, Luke opened his car door and paused,
staring at the building.

"Did you think two years ago that we'd
ever work together on a project like this
again?" he asked, turning to the other man.

Waylon shook his head. "Luke, with you I

never doubted it. The only thing that surprised me was how fast you made it happen."

A sudden, explosive roar blew away Luke's reply. He spun around, staring in disbelief as the entire left side of the building they'd left only minutes before began to crumple. Flames leaped upward, smoke steamed above it. Steel beams and girders, concrete and Sheetrock, tumbled down like a house of cards in a strong wind.

"Holy hell," Luke swore as he pulled Waylon to the ground with him.

One more time his dreams had blown up in his face.

The first sight of a possible bombing scene always hit Alex hard. The Alsobrook Investments Building was no exception. The main portion appeared undamaged, and from that she could see the promise of the uncompleted building. Several fire crews were battling to bring the blaze under control, but it looked as though the fire was contained to one wing of the building.

Picking her way through a crowd of on-lookers, firemen, police, and members of the Dallas County Division of the Bureau of Alcohol, Tobacco and Firearms, she eventually found the first officer on the scene, a beat cop who patrolled the area. "Senior Corporal Alex

Sheridan, bomb unit," she said to him, identifying herself. "Can you fill me in, Officer Crandall? Briefly, for now."

"Sure thing, Detective." Handing her his report, he drew in a breath and plunged into a recitation of the facts. "I arrived on the scene at six thirty-seven P.M. after an eyewitness, the architect as it happens, called nine-one-one reporting an explosion. Seems he and the general contractor were leaving the site just as the blast occurred. The architect called it in on his cellular phone. No deaths reported so far."

"None at all?"

He shook his head. "None. And there's one minor injury not caused by the blast." Succumbing to the heat, which was exacerbated by the still-burning fire, he wiped his shirtsleeve across his perspiring face.

Alex tucked the report under her arm, intending to interview the witnesses herself before she read Crandall's more detailed account. No deaths, she thought, relieved. Given the time of day, that wasn't too surprising, but it certainly made the job more pleasant. "So, no workmen. But isn't there a night watchman?"

"Yes, ma'am, he's the injury. We found him knocked out, tied up, and dumped in a temporary building. Got a bump on his head, is all."

Her eyebrows climbed at that news. So, it hadn't been an accident, she thought. Coupled with the time of day, the removal of the night watchman from danger was a sure sign that the explosion had been deliberate. The exact method of destruction was still anybody's guess. Alex's team would start to work on that as soon as the fire chief allowed them access to the building.

"Neither of the witnesses saw anyone entering or leaving the area," Crandall continued. "You've got my initial interviews with them right there." He gestured at the papers under her arm.

It looked like whoever did it took care not to kill anyone, Alex mused. Not unheard of, but still, interesting. "What about the building's owner? Has he been notified?"

"Yes. He hasn't arrived yet. Lives out of town, according to reports."

She nodded, figuring she'd catch up with him in the morning. A nearby sign read: AL-SOBROOK INVESTMENTS. 2000 A.D. ARCHITEC-TURAL. She'd seen Alsobrook's name in the business section of the papers, but she wasn't familiar with many architectural firms. "The architect and the contractor are the eyewitnesses, you say? Can you point me toward them?" she asked Crandall.

"Right over there," he said, motioning at a couple of men several yards away.

"Thanks, Officer Crandall. I'll get back with you later."

One of the men stood with his back to her,

staring at the ruined building and the activities of the fire crews, she assumed. The man beside him was cussing a blue streak, until he caught sight of Alex walking toward him and stopped in mid-sentence with his mouth hanging open. It wasn't an uncommon reaction, and it never failed to amuse her.

Alex knew that her canary-yellow suit with its slim, short skirt set her apart from the sea of navy and khaki uniforms surrounding her. She didn't look like a cop, and she took full advantage of that effect when questioning people at a crime scene.

People, especially men, were often more candid with a woman—especially one they didn't perceive as a threat. They often let drop a good bit of information they wouldn't have ordinarily given a law officer. At least until they realized that Alex was as professional as any cop or they learned of her reputation within the police community.

"Wow," she heard the man staring at her say, almost reverently. "Who's the babe?"

The other man shrugged his shoulders, his powerful physique not a bit disguised by a baby-blue dress shirt with rolled-up sleeves or the beige cotton slacks he wore. An uncannily familiar build, she thought, also taking note of the thick black hair brushing his collar. A flutter of awareness tickled her senses.

"Thrill seeker," he said, still staring at the wreckage. "They're all over the place."

A deep voice. Gravel with a hint of steel. The voice she'd last heard speaking in seductive murmurs during a still California night. A night of unremitting passion. Nerves beat a drumroll of apprehension in her stomach. *Oh, God, it couldn't be.*

"Doesn't look like it," the other man said. "I think I saw her flash a badge a few minutes ago."

Her steps faltered before she regained control. Imagination, she told herself. She'd been thinking of him recently, after all. Daily, to be honest. But the man standing with his back to her couldn't possibly be—

Luke Morgan turned his head.

THREE

Tornado-dark gray eyes gazed straight into hers. An electrifying jolt of connection drove every hint of breath from her body.

They stared at each other as the silence lengthened, winding tightly between them. People, sounds, smells . . . everything but the two of them faded into oblivion. Unconsciously, Alex reached up to touch her hair, freezing as she saw his eyes glow with the same memory that flooded her mind.

"Your hair . . ." He picked up a heavy strand from where it lay on her bare chest and rubbed it between his fingers. "It's like a prairie sunset. So many shades of red you can't begin to describe it."

Her breath caught as she stared at him. "I didn't know you had such a poetic streak."

His answering smile was pure devil, not a trace of the poet. "Neither did I."

She heard the words whisper clearly in the twilight air, just as she had that night three weeks before.

A man cleared his throat, breaking the silence as effectively as an explosion.

The shock had already faded from Luke's expression. He even looked a little amused. "Hello, Alex. Your case, I take it?"

Thank God she could breathe again. Nodding, she managed to answer him as casually as he'd addressed her, even though her mind was screaming *How?* and *Why him?* and her heart was pounding at Mach speed. "Hello, Luke. How have you been?"

"Fine, until about an hour ago." All trace of amusement left his face when it hardened as if in grim memory.

He'd never let on that he lived in Dallas. But then, she'd never asked. "You're the architect in charge of this project? You work for 2000 A.D. Architectural?"

"Not exactly. I *am* 2000 A.D." He glanced at the building again. "What's left of it. Alex Sheridan, this"—he gestured at the man beside him who'd been darting curious looks at both of them—"is Waylon Black, my general contractor."

"You two know each other?" Black asked.

"We met at a conference," Luke said. The ironic glance he gave Alex reminded her he could have said much more.

Alex pulled out her badge, showing it to both of them, though she felt a little foolish flashing it at Luke. He knew damn well what she did. "Detective Sheridan, Mr. Black," she said at her most professional. "I'm an investigator with the Dallas Police Department Bomb Unit. I'll be working on this case."

Instinctively, she turned to Luke. "Is there someplace we can go to talk? I'm sure you'd prefer not to go downtown yet, though I might need you both to do so at some point."

"Waylon?" Luke raised an eyebrow at him.

"Uh, my office." He waved his hand at a beige tin building some distance from the site of the blast.

"Fine," Alex said. "I'd like to see you one at a time, if I may. Mr. Black?" Starting with him would give her a little more time to get herself under control.

"Sure." Understandably, given the circumstances, he looked shell-shocked himself. "Anything to find out what happened here."

"Don't worry. I intend to."

Without another glance at Luke, she turned her back on him, but it was damned hard to do. Especially when she felt his gaze on her as she walked away. Remember the job, she lectured herself. Forget about any personal relationships. Concentrate on the investigation and worry about everything else later. But she found Luke Morgan extremely distracting. She had a feeling she would have even without their encounter three weeks before.

Black's brief description of the event concurred with what he'd told Officer Crandall. It didn't shed much light on who might have set the bomb, but Alex hadn't expected it to. Her customary list of questions brought no surprise answers and Black could think of no reason anyone would want the building demolished. In fact, he had to be convinced that the explosion had been deliberate and not an accident.

"Considering what happened to the night watchman," she said, "it appears to have been intentional."

"You mean because he was coshed on the head?"

"Because someone took the time to make sure he wasn't in the building when it exploded."

Black cursed and gazed out the window, running a hand through his spiky brown hair. Alex remained silent, doing what she did best. Watching. Waiting. After a time, he muttered, "This is going to kill Luke. Dammit, it's not right."

That got her attention. "Mr. Morgan? Why? Isn't he insured?"

Black snorted. "Sure. But the insurance company won't be in any hurry to settle this claim. Especially if you're right and it was a bomb. This is about the worst thing that could have happened to Luke right now, with him finally getting back into—" He broke off abruptly.

When he didn't finish, she let it go and asked another question. "Was Mr. Morgan with you the entire meeting?"

"Yeah. Why?"

She didn't answer for a moment, waiting for his dawning comprehension. "As the architect, Mr. Morgan would be in a position—"

Scowling, Black cut her off. "That's crap. Luke Morgan would no more blow up that building than I would."

It didn't seem to occur to him that she might think he'd done it. Letting the subject of Luke drop, she continued with her questions. "Do you know of anyone with a grudge against you? Any of your crew?"

He was shaking his head. "No, nothing like that. Me and my crew get along real good."

Did they? she wondered. It was something to check out. She'd also check on how well he got along with Luke Morgan. Could be his defense of Luke was a smoke screen. "How about Mr. Morgan, then? Does he have any rivals that you know of? Any enemies who might see this as a way to get back at him for something? Is that a possibility in your opinion?"

"Yeah, I guess." He shrugged. "But I don't know who. Not anymore."

She thought it a strange statement, but al-

lowed him to leave, fairly certain she'd get no
more of use from Waylon Black at the current
time. She waited, trying to compose herself
and her thoughts in preparation to seeing Luke
Morgan again. She wasn't very successful.

A minute later, he strode into the room,
halting in front of the desk and looking down
at her with an enigmatic expression. She barely
contained the curse that rose to her lips. He
looked good, even better than she remembered, and the shadows of strain darkening his
eyes and stretching his mouth into a grim, hard
line only added to his dangerous appeal.

It hadn't all been moonlight and vulnerability, she admitted. Staring at him, Alex realized
that she was as attracted to him now, under the
harsh glare of phosphorescent lights and in
highly stressful circumstances, as she'd been on
that reckless, moonlit night three weeks ago.

Dammit! Why did Luke Morgan have to be
involved in the case? She was in charge of a
bomb investigation, dealing with a possible
suspect who'd both literally and figuratively
seen her naked. Of the two, she'd much rather
he'd seen only her body, and not into her mind
as well.

"You didn't know I lived in Dallas," he said,
breaking the silence that stretched between
them like a trip wire.

"Ah—no. No, I didn't." She looked down,
rearranging her papers restlessly.

"I didn't think the next time I saw you we'd be talking about explosions. Not this kind, anyway."

Her head snapped up. Giving herself a mental slap, she drew in her breath and spoke in an ice-cool tone. "Let's get one thing clear before we begin this interview. I'm here as an investigator. Nothing else."

He studied her for a moment, then took a seat. "Understood. But before I start answering questions, I've got a few of my own."

She raised an eyebrow at his peremptory tone. "Such as?"

"Was anyone injured or killed? I saw Fred, the night watchman, and I know he's okay, but I haven't been able to find out if anyone else was around. The cops wouldn't say much."

Alex saw no harm in telling him. "As far as we know, there were no casualties."

"Thank God for something, anyway," he said, and settled back in his chair. "All right. Fire away."

Quelling the urge to shake him for his word choice, she reminded herself that he'd just witnessed a violent explosion, one that could have easily killed him, and thus deserved her sympathy. The routine of questioning would settle her nerves. She hoped.

"Let's start from the beginning," she said.

Luke's basic story was the same as the general contractor's. Neither man had seen a bomber or anyone else. Nor, since they hadn't been looking at the building, had they seen any fire or smoke just before the explosion.

When she began asking questions about the sound the bomb made, the color and size of the fireball, the color and amount of the smoke, Luke surprised her by his detailed descriptions. Far more in-depth than Waylon Black's answers had been.

"You're extremely observant," she said, leaving a faint question in her tone. "These descriptions should be quite helpful in determining what caused the explosion."

He shrugged. "I make my living noticing details."

That was true, she imagined. Still, his answers had been more on the order of a trained observer than a typical witness. But he wasn't a typical witness. At least not to her. She was all too aware of him as a man. Worse, she was conscious of him as a lover.

The knowledge stung her, stirring up her anger and frustration. "What effect will the explosion have on your architectural firm?"

"Not a good one. I'll be lucky if it doesn't ruin me."

Hands on the desktop, she steepled her fingers. "You seem very calm about that."

"Calm? No," he said grimly. "I've had the foundation knocked out from under me before. Becoming hysterical isn't an asset."

The image of a hysterical Luke Morgan wouldn't gel. "Not everyone has your . . ." She let the sentence hang a long moment and finished, "Your composure."

His eyes narrowed. "Are you getting at something, Alex?"

"Such as?"

"Such as implying I'm a suspect?"

She lifted one shoulder indifferently, though his blunt question had surprised her. "No more so than anyone else. At this point, anyone with a connection to the Alsobrook Investments Building will be investigated. Anyone," she repeated, letting her gaze linger impassively on his face.

His eyes had hardened to a flinty gray and the line of his jaw looked as solid as a concrete post. She realized she'd finally pierced that unnatural calm of his. Luke Morgan was mad as hell. She'd bet her next paycheck on it.

"Nail the bastard," homicide Detective Lieutenant Nicholas Sheridan was saying as Alex walked into his office later that evening. "Yeah, right." He slammed the phone down and heaved a satisfied sign before looking at her. "I love it when we catch the bad guy."

"Don't we all," she said. "Got a minute, Nick?" She picked through the remains of the pizza box that lay open on her brother's desk.

A piece of crust, an olive, and a pepperoni slice didn't do much for her, so she flipped the top to cover it. Shoving the box aside, she leaned a hip on the edge of his desk and parked herself there.

"For you, I've got two. What's up, sis?"

Alex hesitated, unsure how to begin. For one thing, although she was close to her brother, she had absolutely no intention of discussing her love life with him. But she had to talk to someone and Nick usually gave good advice. "Have you ever had a case that you weren't sure you could be objective about?"

"Sure, all the time. Had one just the other day." He crumpled up a piece of paper and shot it at the trash can in the corner. "Guy blew away his kid because—"

"Not that kind of nonobjective," Alex interrupted. "I mean a case where you know one of the suspects. Or possible suspects," she amended.

Nick leaned back in his chair and swung his feet up onto the desk. "One time I knew a snitch who took out another snitch. But that's not what you're talking about, is it?" Alex shook her head, and he went on: "Why are you afraid you can't be objective? Is it someone you know well?"

Yes and no, she thought. "Sort of. Somebody I was, um, kind of involved with."

He laced his hands behind his head and

gave her an indulgent smile. "Pick some winners, don't you?"

"You're one to talk," she fired back. "Most of the women you date have an IQ equal to half their bra size."

"I don't date 'em for their brains, honey," he said, grinning. "But I haven't dated a suspect in a bombing, either. That's what you're asking about, isn't it? That bomb that went off earlier this afternoon is yours, I take it."

"Yes, it's mine. And I didn't date him. Exactly." No, she'd just had an incredible one-night stand with him, but she didn't want to tell Nick that. "He wasn't a suspect then. Besides, he's only a possible suspect."

Her brother was staring at her like she'd lost her mind. "I don't think I want you to clarify that for me."

"Good, because I'm not going to."

"What are you doing here anyway?" Nick asked. "Why aren't you still at the bomb site?"

"Damned conscientious fire chief won't let us near it until he's got things more under control. I decided I might as well do some paperwork and go back later." She'd gone a few rounds with the fire chief before, so rather than fight a futile battle, she'd opted to leave. Reminded of her frustration, she scowled at Nick as she'd wanted to do at the fire chief. "What I need from you is to tell me how to deal with this."

He shrugged. "Give it to someone else. Your captain will understand."

"No. This is my case, I should be able to handle it." She shoved herself away to pace the small office. "I can do this. All I have to do is be professional. That's it, professional." She whirled and demanded, "Right?"

Nick spread his hands. "Whatever you say."

"I'll simply forget I ever knew him and . . ." Her voice trailed off. Forget that night? Fat chance. "It doesn't matter," she said, drawing herself up and pinning her brother with a sharp glare. "Do you think I can't do my job? Well, I can. I can do whatever it takes."

"Oh, absolutely."

She slapped her palm down on his desk. "He's not going to get to me. I won't let him."

"Hate to tell you, Alex, but it sounds to me like he already has."

Nick was right, dammit, but she wouldn't admit it. She couldn't afford to let anything that had happened that night affect her investigation.

"By the way," he went on, "I've been racking my brain to think of which of your former boyfriends might be a bomber in disguise and I just can't figure it. So, who is it?"

"You don't know him. I only met him recently."

Nick lifted an eyebrow. "Must have been pretty damn recent. You haven't been involved with anyone in five years, as far as I know. Not seriously, anyway."

She shot him a dirty look. "Back off, Nick. You don't want to know the details, I promise."

He studied her for a long moment. "Could be you're right. I don't think I do."

"What would you do if you were in this situation?"

"If you're not going to give the case to someone else, then I've got one word of advice. Compartmentalize."

Compartmentalize? That was it? "Meaning what?"

"Take whatever happened between you and this guy and lock it away. Put it out of your mind. Then do your job."

Lock it away. Do her job. She could manage that. She had no other choice. And if it meant putting a dark-haired temptation out of her mind, then by God, that's what she'd do.

FOUR

"I'm sorry, sir," the uniformed cop told Luke, "you'll need permission before you can enter."

Luke glanced again at the rubble that had once been a wing of a beautiful building and grimaced. The breaking sun illuminated the grisly scene with an eerie glow. His grip tightened on the hard hat in his hand. "Dammit, I want to see the damage. What do you think I'm going to do, blow it up again?"

"I couldn't say, sir. But you can't enter the premises until you get—"

Luke cut him off. "Permission. Yeah, I heard you the first two times. Whose permission do I need?"

"Mine, for a start," a husky female voice said from behind him.

He turned and found himself staring into

Senior Corporal Alex Sheridan's beautiful blue eyes. She sounded like she'd just crawled out of bed, but from the looks of her, she hadn't been to sleep yet. She wore the same clothes she'd had on the day before, a canary-yellow suit now sporting liberal patches of grime, though she'd exchanged her high heels for steel-toed boots. She held a pair of protective gloves in one hand and a hard hat in the other. Soot smudged her cheeks, shadows plagued her eyes, and she was still gorgeous enough to haunt a man's dreams.

Alex Sheridan looked, he thought, like she should be some rich man's plaything, not a working cop. And it annoyed the hell out of him that he even noticed her looks when his career was lying in ruins a few feet away.

"I'm glad you're here," she continued. "I need to ask you some further questions."

The midnight timbre of her voice made him think of sex and sin rather than explosions and buildings. That irritated the hell out of him as well. "Ask anything you want as long as you let me in there," he said, jerking his head at the scene of destruction.

She lifted one eyebrow in cool question. "Why do you want to go in?"

"So I can begin to assess the damage to the building. I need to take some notes, see how much damage there is in order to discuss it with my team of engineers. The owner wants to know whether it's salvageable or if the entire structure will have to come down."

"I'm afraid no one—"

He threw a hand up in frustration. "Dammit, Alex, don't give me that official-line garbage. This is my career we're talking about. Is it so much to ask?"

Frowning, she glanced at the building, then back to him. "I can't just turn you loose here."

"Then don't. Come with me. You can ask me all the questions you want, but at least let me do something useful while we're talking."

She appeared to be debating his suggestion. After a long moment, she sighed. "All right. But you'll have to be content with the main building for now. Members of the bomb unit are still investigating the actual blast area and it hasn't been deemed safe for civilians yet."

He nodded. "I want access to that wing as soon as possible."

"You and half of Texas. The insurance companies are here too." She walked toward the entrance.

Slapping his hat on, he followed her. "Have you established the cause of the explosion?"

"Yes. Definitely an improvised explosive device. An IED, we call them. In layman's terms, a bomb. We found the explosive mechanism early this morning."

The muscles in his jaw tightened, his right

hand clenched into a fist. "I wish I had just two minutes alone with the bomber."

As they reached the entrance Alex put on her hard hat and turned to look at him. "Where do you want to start?"

"Main floor, as close to the wreckage as we can get. I need to get an idea of how much harm was done to the entire structure, and how much was confined to the area of the blast. It's possible that we'll only lose the one wing." If they were lucky. If they weren't, then the whole thing would have to come down. And in that case, who knew if it would be rebuilt?

"I'd like to know your whereabouts yesterday," Alex said, breaking in on his grim thoughts. "Beginning in the morning, please." She'd pulled a small notebook and a pen from somewhere and waited for his answers.

"I was in my office from seven-thirty A.M. until about five or five-fifteen. At five-thirty, I met here with Waylon Black." Glancing around the entryway, Luke felt hopeful that at least on the surface it appeared undamaged. Nothing certain would be known, though, until he brought his team in to test for structural damage.

"You met here? In the building itself or the temporary office?"

"Both. We toured the building, then talked some more in his office." He squatted down to look more closely at a wall that had buckled.

"Were you constantly in Mr. Black's company? Did he leave you at any time during the meeting?"

Rising, Luke stared at her. "No, we were together the entire time. Why? Are you implying—"

"I'm not implying anything. I'm asking questions."

"Waylon Black didn't plant that bomb. That's not the way he operates."

"I'm sure he'll appreciate the vote of confidence," she said, "since he gave you the same one."

Luke struggled with his temper. She'd made it obvious she considered him a suspect, but hearing that she'd discussed it with Waylon brought it home to him.

"Now, let's talk insurance," she said in a tone that had him gritting his teeth. "Do you hold insurance on the structure or do you only have errors-and-omissions insurance?"

"Both. I'm named as additional insured on the contractor's builder's risk insurance. It's not enough to set me up in Tahiti for life," he added sarcastically. "You're welcome to check it out, though."

"Don't worry, I intend to." She asked him a few more general questions, making notes as she did. "Do you know of any individual or organization who might be responsible for this explosion?"

"Not terrorists," he said, thinking aloud. Far too low-key for a terrorist organization. Besides, somebody would have claimed credit for the bombing and it would have been smeared all over the news by this time.

"Why do you say that?" Her tone had sharpened with the question.

Glancing at her, he saw she was staring intently at him. "No deaths. Not gory enough for them. Not enough bang for their buck, so to speak." After a moment, he added, "But you should know that better than I do."

She nodded. "I agree it's unlikely to be the work of a terrorist group."

"Great. So you don't think it's terrorists. Do you have any ideas as to who it might be?" It hadn't even been a day, he reminded himself, but he couldn't quite curb his impatience to have the situation resolved. And to have himself taken off the list of suspects.

"A few. We're working on it," she said, unruffled by his tone. "Do you have any business rival who might have it in for you? Any enemies?"

"Most of my enemies are dead."

"How fortunate for you," she said dryly. "So there's no one you can think of."

Though he understood she was only doing her job, her questions, and even more her impersonal manner, were beginning to jerk his chain. His jaw clenched and it took him a moment to answer. "No. And I don't see Waylon Black having many enemies. Maybe Alsobrook has some."

"Perhaps. I haven't talked with him yet. Do you know what kind of insurance the owner holds?"

Luke stalked through an open doorway into a hallway and ran his hand down the wall, feeling for cracks. "Why do you keep harping on the insurance? God knows that money will take forever to come through."

"But it will come through eventually."

"You think somebody blew it up for the insurance money."

"I think it's a possibility."

She's a cop, he reminded himself, who was doing her job. "The insurance companies won't give us a dime until you find out who did it."

She glanced down at her notes. "Then you won't mind cooperating with the police," she said, her voice totally dispassionate.

He stopped inspecting the wall and glared at her. "What the hell do you think I've been doing?"

She looked up at him without speaking, her expression bland and neutral, pen poised over the notebook. As if she didn't know him at all instead of having spent a wild night of passion in his arms. He wondered what it would take to disrupt that calm air of hers. Rather than shake her, which he was sorely tempted to do, he turned his back on her.

"Do you know of anything else that might be pertinent to the investigation?"

His temper snapped at her words. Turning swiftly, he reached her side in two strides and leveled a hard stare at her. "Luke," he said through gritted teeth.

"I beg your pardon?"

"You seem to have forgotten my name."

Her eyes widened, her breath drew in with a sharp hiss. "I—no, I hadn't forgotten."

"But you're doing your best to, aren't you?" He reached out and traced the fragile line of her jaw with his fingers. Her skin was soft, as soft as it had been that night three weeks ago. And every bit as tempting, dammit. "A shame I had the bad taste to be involved in one of your cases, isn't it?"

Her eyes flashed fire as he finally broke through her indifference. "Don't be ridiculous." She jerked her head away from him. "I'm simply doing my job."

"You're simply treating me like we've never met, much less spent—"

She slapped her hand on his chest, cutting him off in mid-sentence. "Don't bring that up! This is a professional situation and that—that night has no bearing on anything."

"So you do remember. I was beginning to wonder if you had selective amnesia." They glared at each other, her eyes a stormy blue, her breath coming fast. "Dammit, this ought to remind you," he muttered, and jerked her to him to kiss her.

Maybe it was shock that had her lips parting and her tongue answering his, but in the moment he held her crushed against him, his mouth hard and hungry on hers, he felt her body's ardent response. Then she went rigid. Her other hand came up between them and she shoved him backward. Having proved his point, Luke let her go.

Chest heaving, temper sparking in her eyes and flooding her cheeks with color, she faced him. "Do that again and I'll slap your tail in jail so fast, it will make your head spin."

Genuinely amused, he laughed. "You're going to throw me in jail for kissing you? A bit of an overreaction, don't you think?"

Still furious, she glared at him. "I remember," she said, her voice so low, he had to strain to hear it. "But I don't want to discuss it. This is an official investigation and I'd like to get on with it."

He searched her face, wondering why she was so determined to bury that night. "Fine. We'll discuss it later. When you're not *officially investigating.*"

"There's nothing to discuss."

"Like hell there's not. But we'll leave it for later."

For a minute he thought she would argue, but she merely retrieved her notebook from where it had fallen and began perusing her notes. He noticed, though, that her hands weren't quite steady, which gave him a small measure of satisfaction.

"We're almost through, for now. But you didn't answer my question. Do you know anything else that might be pertinent to the investigation?"

Good investigators didn't give up, he thought. "No." Nothing he was interested in telling her, anyway. She'd find out soon enough when she checked him out.

Which, he knew, she would.

Late that afternoon back at the station, Alex buried her face in her hands, wishing she had time for even a half-hour catnap. Her eyes felt gritty from lack of sleep, she was filthy and exhausted from crawling around in the ruins of the Alsobrook building, and she was still reeling from seeing Luke Morgan again. He unsettled her more every time she was with him.

So much for remaining professional and detached.

The problem was, she acknowledged, she didn't want Luke to be guilty. And to be honest, Waylon Black was a better bet as a suspect than Luke. Not that she wanted to pin the crime on the contractor or Henry Alsobrook or anyone else. But she really didn't want to find out that Luke had set that bomb. So was she overreacting, as he'd accused her of doing? Trying to prove his guilt because she was unsure of her own motives?

Casting her mind back, she saw Luke's face as they viewed the damage. His expression had been grim and, she could have sworn, pained. He hadn't looked like a man who was seeing dollar signs at the prospect of additional fees; he'd looked like a man in a world of hurt. Her instincts told her that Luke Morgan hadn't blown up that building.

Her instincts had been wrong before.

Her partner Jenna had died proving that.

Alex had known Jenna wasn't prepared—no matter that she'd completed the training. If only Alex had gone herself . . . But she hadn't.

If Jenna hadn't touched that right rear door, would the car have still exploded? Jenna had only done what they'd all been trained to do. Would Alex herself have acted any differently? Would her instincts have kicked in if she'd been the one approaching the car, or had it been fear for her partner that had triggered her alarm? Alex didn't know. Would never know.

Oh, God, she didn't want to rehash the past another futile time. Attempting to stem the headache, she rubbed her throbbing temples. There were never answers, only guilt. And Alex was tired, so damn tired of the guilt.

Her past wasn't the issue here. But Luke Morgan's past was another matter. She'd already run a criminal history on him and found nothing. His driver's-license check hadn't even turned up a lousy parking violation. Wondering if he'd spent time in the military, she decided to put in a call to the National Personnel Records Center in St. Louis.

Luckily, she had a personal contact at the center who agreed to search for the information while Alex waited on the line. Even pursuant to an investigation, the records weren't always so quickly available.

It wasn't fair to convict the man because she was afraid to admit she had feelings for him. She closed her eyes and felt his lips on hers, felt herself melting against him, wanting more. . . . Until she'd remembered that they were standing in the ruins of a bombed-out building, for God's sake, and he was a suspect.

"Detective Sheridan?" her contact said, interrupting her musing.

"Yes, I'm here."

"I've got a copy of his service records right here. I'll fax it to you as soon as we're finished talking, but I thought you'd like to know he served seven years with the navy, the last five as a SEAL."

"A SEAL?" she blurted out.

"That's right." Papers rustled as the clerk paused. "A demolitions specialist."

Stomach rolling, hands shaking, Alex hung up the phone. Luke Morgan had been a navy SEAL—and an expert in demolitions.

Demolitions.

Great instincts, Alex. Just great.

FIVE

"That damned female thinks *I'm* the one who planted that damned bomb in that damned building!" Waylon shouted, stomping into Luke's office the next afternoon and slamming the door shut behind him.

Luke looked up from the blueprints spread out in front of him. "Yeah, I know."

"Well, by God." Waylon pounded his fist on Luke's desk so hard that a coffee mug jumped. "I didn't do it and I resent the hell out of some prissy cop acting like I did."

Luke's lips twitched at the description. "Not prissy, Waylon. Definitely not prissy. And don't take it so hard. She suspects me too."

He snorted. "Not as much as she does me, I'll bet. Besides, you said you knew her." Pausing for breath, he studied Luke. "Just how well do you know this woman?"

"Forget it, Waylon."

"That well, huh?" He slid Luke a sly glance. "She's a looker, all right."

"Alex Sheridan is a cop," Luke said, irritated at his friend for reasons he didn't care to examine. "And she's just doing her job." Why was he defending Alex to Waylon? He'd been just as angry to realize that she suspected him. Angrier, in fact. "We should have known we'd be the first people the cops would look at."

"Why? Because we were there when it blew?"

"That's one reason. And face it, if Alsobrook rebuilds, both of us stand to gain. Not only in insurance but in fees." Alex had no way of knowing that it would be much better for Luke's career to get the project finished and the building occupied instead of making more money from additional fees. Luke wasn't after the quick money; he was far more concerned with the long-term growth of his business.

"For what it's worth," he added, "I told her you didn't do it. Not that she appeared to be listening to me."

"The woman grilled me about insurance for half an hour." Waylon propped his hands on his hips and glared at Luke as if it were his fault. "Must have asked me the same questions five times. Guess she was trying to see if I'd change my story. Kept asking me if I had any beefs with you or Alsobrook too."

"It's routine. Relax. Neither of us did it, so it shouldn't make any difference what she asks." But it did. What Alex did, and what she thought, mattered to him on an intensely personal level.

He was damned if he knew why he wanted so much for her to believe his innocence. Obviously, it was important given that she was the detective in charge of the investigation, but it was more than that. Why did he feel a connection with this woman? Even more puzzling, why did he want one?

"Yeah, maybe you're right," Waylon said. "Got sidetracked there. Dadburned woman." He shoved his hands through his hair. "I came over to see if you have any idea when we'll start up construction again. Thing is, I've got another job I've been putting off. A little one. Shouldn't take but two or three weeks."

"Since my team of engineers hasn't been allowed in yet, there's no telling how long it will be before we need your full crew again. Go ahead and take that job."

"Figured you'd say that. Thanks." He started to leave, pausing at the door. "I hope to hell that Detective Sheridan knows what she's doing and finds the guy who did it soon. I don't much care to go to prison for something I didn't do. Catch you later."

The door slammed shut behind him, not because he was angry this time, Luke knew, but because Waylon always left with a bang. It was an idiosyncrasy that had taken some getting used to.

He reached down to pick up the envelope that had fallen to the floor with Waylon's exit. Something from the bank, he noticed, remembering that he'd seen it the day before but had been too busy and too distracted to open it. It must have gotten buried beneath the blueprints. He started to toss it back on his desk, then shrugged and ripped it open instead.

A single piece of paper fluttered to the desktop. A deposit slip for his corporate account. He picked it up, looking at it more closely.

One hundred thousand dollars had been electronically transferred into his account.

And he had no idea who had done it.

Alex was on her way out when the dispatcher called her back. "Phone for you, Detective Sheridan. Says he won't talk to anyone else."

Though she wanted nothing more at the moment than to go home and digest the rest of the information she'd managed to dig up on Luke Morgan, she answered it. Time to think, that was what she needed. But you could never tell when a witness might come forward and Alex had a feeling she needed all the help she could get on her newest case.

"Alex Sheridan."

"Something's happened that I think you'll be interested in hearing about."

"Luke?" Of course it was him. She'd recognize that gorgeous voice anywhere.

"My place. I'm sure you've got the address in your files." With that he hung up.

Enraged at his calm assumption that she not only knew his voice but that she'd do his bidding, Alex jerked the receiver away from her ear and stared at it. It would serve him right if she had him hauled in. She was tempted, very tempted, to do just that.

Maybe he intended to come clean about his background. But she couldn't see why he would do so now when he hadn't earlier. He had to have known she'd discover not only his military service but his work history as well.

Accounts of his previous architectural firm were public record. Alex had spent the day reading about Morgan & Bennett. About James Bennett's indictment for fraud and for bribing a public official, the near bankruptcy of the firm, and its subsequent dissolution.

She wondered how, or even if, those factors played into the bombing. More, she wanted to know how it had affected Luke and how he'd come back from disaster in such a short time.

Alex decided not to bring him down to the station because she knew he wouldn't talk if she did. At least, that's what she told herself, but she had an uneasy feeling that wasn't her only motive.

Half an hour later, she stood in his apartment, thinking how well it suited him. Very much a man's domain, with bold, earthy colors and comfortable yet elegant furniture. Nothing frilly, frivolous, or feminine about it. She wouldn't have said it lacked a woman's touch. It didn't need one. It was simply and completely Luke's.

"Can I get you something to drink?"

He was dressed casually, she noticed, in faded jeans, worn white at the stress points. A black short-sleeved T-shirt stretched snugly across his broad chest. Unbidden came the memory of what that beautifully muscled chest had looked like shirtless.

Angry at her errant thoughts, she snapped, "This isn't a social call."

He smiled at her, an infuriatingly sexy smile, his gaze slowly skimming over her body. A vision of what had happened the last time he'd looked at her that way danced in her mind. Ruthlessly, she pushed it out.

"I'm only offering a glass of iced tea, Alex."

Feeling foolish, she nodded. "All right. Thanks." Trust him immediately to put her at a disadvantage.

While he disappeared into the kitchen she took a seat, perching on the edge of an overstuffed burgundy leather easy chair. Luke came into the living room a moment later and set a tall frosted glass before her on the coffee table.

"You have information for me, I take it? Concerning the investigation?" To settle the annoying burst of nerves—and memories—she sipped her tea.

"Something happened today that I think you need to know about." He handed her a piece of paper, standing beside her while she looked at it.

A bank deposit slip on Luke Morgan's account, she saw. For one hundred thousand dollars.

Dated two days before the bombing.

She looked up at him. His jaw muscles had tightened and his eyes had hardened to a steely gray. He met her gaze, but said nothing. Waiting, she supposed, for her response. "Interesting," she said, striving to keep her voice bland, though all her instincts had gone on red alert. "But why show it to me?"

"Because I think someone is trying to frame me. Or at the least, throw suspicion on me."

"The reason being . . ." She let her voice trail off, waiting for him to finish the sentence.

"Come on, Alex." He started to pace, stalking the room with energy and not a little anger.

"A large amount of money—money I can't explain—appears in my bank account two days before the Alsobrook building blows up. What's your first thought? As an investigator."

"That you were paid to plant the bomb." She folded her hands together and watched him.

"Right." He threw one hand up in a frustrated gesture. "So here I am, prime suspect in the bombing. Worse, I have no idea who made that deposit. All I've been able to find out from my bank is that it was an electronic transfer from First Bank of St. Thomas in the Virgin Islands."

"And you know nothing else about it."

"Nothing," he said over his shoulder, still pacing. "Mail hasn't been high on my priorities lately. I've pretty much put everything but this disaster on the back burner. If I hadn't opened the envelope by chance today, I still wouldn't know about it. But I'll tell you this. I may not know *who* made that deposit, but I've got a damned good idea of *why* they made it. Somebody blew up my best project and now they're trying to frame me for the crime."

"What exactly are you asking me to do?"

"Investigate it. You can find out more from the banks than I can, and besides that, it will help you too." He halted in front of her. "Think about it, Alex. You asked if I had any enemies. Apparently I do. Someone is trying very hard to wreck my life. And they're doing a damned good job of it."

She had to admit his theory made sense. If she'd found out about the deposit on her own later in the investigation, it would have looked very damning for him. Besides, if he'd been paid that kind of money, why would he put it into an account the police could easily access? Why wouldn't he have put it in a hidden account?

Unless he was playing some convoluted game that she hadn't figured out yet. "Assuming what you're saying is true—"

"Why the hell would I tell you about this otherwise? Do I look that stupid?"

No, but he might be that smart, she thought, deciding to press further. "If you're innocent, then why didn't you come clean about your background? Care to explain the matter of your military service, Lieutenant Morgan?"

He hesitated briefly, then shrugged. "What's to explain? You've obviously seen my records. You know I was a navy SEAL. So what?"

"I asked you if you had any information that might be pertinent to this investigation. Didn't it occur to you that I might be interested in knowing not only that you were a SEAL, but that you were your team's top explosives specialist?"

"My military service is public record. I didn't tell you because it doesn't matter a damn what my background is."

"Perhaps not on its own, but added to this"—she tapped a finger on the deposit slip lying on the coffee table—"things aren't looking good for you."

His hands clenched into fists. She could see that it cost him to answer her calmly. "I didn't blow up the Alsobrook building. You're focusing your energy, and your suspicions, on the wrong person. Have you even looked at anyone else's background?"

She met his gaze as calmly as she could. "My team is investigating all the possibilities."

"Is that so? Seems to me you've been too busy trying to bust my ass to have had time to check out anyone else. You want to tell me why?"

"I'm simply doing my jo—"

A choice expletive cut her off. Reaching down, he grabbed her wrist and yanked her to her feet. "I've had enough. Let's lay it out on the table, Alex. You want to nail my hide to the wall. Are you going to tell me why?"

She struggled to break his grip, but couldn't. "That's not true. I don't." He held her fast, her fist against his chest, forcing her to stand so close, she could feel the anger steaming from him, see it smoldering in his eyes.

"Yes, you do." His voice deepened, quieted.

His fingers around her wrist gentled, though he didn't let go. The anger became banked as something else took its place. Something raw . . . and frightening. "Because of the night we spent together. That night has you running scared."

"You don't know what you're talking about." Her heart sprinted, fear, anger, denial battling inside her. "That night has nothing to do with any of this. It was a one-night stand. That's all."

"It was more."

"No."

"It could be more still."

"No." She shook her head, denying it, denying him. "I can't. Don't you get it? I can't! You're a—" She stopped talking abruptly.

He pulled her even closer. "A suspect. And that makes me off-limits. That makes it easier for you. You don't want to believe I'm innocent, do you? Because then you'd have to deal with me on an emotional level."

"Oh, that must be it, Sigmund," she snapped, attempting to gain the upper hand. She couldn't let him know what he did to her. How he made her feel, and even worse, how much he made her want. She couldn't let the confusion take control.

"You know what's really getting to you?" He released her hand and touched her cheek, stroked his fingers over it, over her mouth. "I know your weakness."

She clamped her lips together to keep them from trembling.

"I know you're not all badass investigator." His hand slid to her neck, caressing it.

She wanted desperately to move, but his voice pinned her, mesmerized her like a thief balking at the wail of the siren.

His voice deepened another level, sending tingles of sensation along her spine. "I've seen the woman beneath—the one who feels passion, the one who feels pain. The woman who cries, who wakes up sweating from nightmares. And you can't stand it. You're not upset because you believe I'm guilty. You're mad as hell because you know I'm innocent."

Anger—and fear that he was right—broke the spell. "Shut up!" She started to slap him, anything to make the words stop. Anything to halt this jumble of emotion.

His hand shot out and gripped her wrist again. She didn't try to jerk free. It was as if she wanted him to . . . what? What did she want? Him to overpower her, force her to admit things . . . things she couldn't admit. Not to him, not to herself.

Luke shook his head, but he didn't shout at her, didn't draw her closer, didn't lower his head to hers. Didn't do any of the things she'd thought he would.

He said, very softly, "Kiss me, Alex, and then tell me you feel nothing. Tell me you don't remember that something else, something that was more than sex, happened between us that night. Then tell me I'm only a suspect to you, nothing more, nothing less."

"Damn you." She wanted to scream at him; instead it was a whisper. His eyes were storm-cloud dark, and God help her, hurting.

Hurting—just as she had been that night in San Diego.

"Yeah. I am damned," he said. "Unless you help me."

SIX

The look in his eyes did her in.

Help him, he'd said. How hard was it for him to ask her that? He had helped her, that night in San Diego. Had chased away the nightmare and, for a time, allowed her peace. She wanted to help him. And she couldn't deny any longer that she simply wanted him.

He said nothing more, nor did she. Her hand lifted to his face, traced his jaw, slid into his black, silky hair. She brought his head down to hers as she rose on her toes, keeping their gazes locked. Then she pressed her mouth to his and kissed him.

The first taste of him snapped her control like an electric shock. She hadn't realized what it would feel like to kiss him, really kiss him again. Hadn't looked for the sledgehammer jolt of desire, or the dizzying wave of tenderness that rolled through her at the same time. How could she feel so strongly about a man she hardly knew?

She kissed him harder, slipping her tongue inside his mouth, reacquainting herself with his taste, his touch, his smell. A groan ripped from his throat, his arms banded tightly around her, crushing her against his chest, and suddenly he was kissing her. His hand moved up her back, cupped her head, and angled her mouth to accept the slow thrust of his tongue, the firm, knowing movements of his lips over hers.

It lasted forever, or seemed to, until it wasn't only a kiss but a revelation as well. Her mind might not be sure of what to make of Luke Morgan, but her body knew exactly what it wanted. Him. To make love with him.

He drew back and stared into her eyes, his own charcoal dark and filled with desire. His voice was a deep rumble, a gravel-and-steel mixture she'd heard in her dreams for three long, empty weeks. "I've thought about you— about this—every day. I didn't want to, but I had no choice. I couldn't forget that night. I couldn't forget you."

He took her mouth again, sipping, feasting, sending rioting throbs of sensation to every part of her body. Need exploding within her, she twined her arms around his neck and gave herself up to the stroke of his tongue, the glide of his hands.

A tiny island of sanity remained in her mind, commanding her to stop, to wait, to think. In an effort to calm her speeding heartbeat, she broke the kiss. Then she felt his hot, open mouth pressed to her hammering pulse and nothing mattered but having his hands on her. Everywhere.

"Wait," she moaned, a last desperate attempt. "Wait, I need to think." But even as she said it she was jerking his shirt from his jeans, running her hands up under it, finally touching his warm, hard chest.

He dragged her against him, cupping her bottom, pulling one leg around his hip. "Think about this," he said, raising her up so she felt the full strength of his arousal pressing against her. "About how much I want you."

All that did was cloud her already muddled mind with heat. "This has nothing to do with"—she gasped, trying to get rid of his shirt and still keep her lower body pressed against his—"the investigation."

"I know." He let her slide down him slowly, so that they each felt her descent, and began to unfasten her buttons. Reaching the last, he spread her blouse open and placed his hands over her breasts. "I know." He kissed her mouth again, his tongue exploring the depths, drawing hers to mate with his. They both groaned when he caressed her.

"I mean it—" Her breath hissed in as he

unfastened her bra clasp and she felt his hands on her naked skin. "This is"—she opened the top button of his jeans—"a separate issue."

"Whatever you say." His words were muffled since he spoke between kisses strung along her neck.

Her nipples tightened against his palms as he rubbed them, an ache spreading through her. She finished wrenching open the fly of his jeans and her gaze collided with his. They were both panting, gulping in air like they'd just run a marathon.

"For God's sake, Alex," he said hoarsely, "let me take you to bed."

"You'd better." She kissed his mouth, quick and hard. "Or I'll have to hurt you."

"You're killing me now," he said, before his mouth came down on hers and took her under.

They stumbled through the room, oblivious to obstacles, stripping clothes between fevered kisses. He tumbled her onto her back across his bed, reaching beneath her skirt to rid her of hose and panties at the same time. Desire burned, licked a flame in her blood as she watched him shove his jeans and briefs down over his hips and step out of them.

Her gaze swept from the shock of dark hair falling over his forehead, to the chiseled mouth that imparted such incredible pleasure, and continued down, drinking in every powerful, masculine inch of him. He was beautiful. And for the moment at least, he was all hers.

"Hurry," was all she could think of to say.

He jerked open the drawer of his bedside table. "Dammit," he muttered, scrambling through it. "I know there are some in here. There have to be."

Alex shimmied out of her skirt. "Luke. Hurry," she said again, her voice husky, throaty. She sprawled naked on his bed, wanting him so much, she thought she might scream if she didn't have him soon.

He turned his head to look at her. His hand froze. "There'd better be some in here," he said hoarsely, "or we're in deep trouble."

She smiled, feeling wicked and wanton and on fire with impatience.

"Hallelujah," he said a moment later, pulling out a packet and ripping it open.

Her pulse pounding, she watched as he rolled the condom down to cover his full length. A strangled groan escaped her and he looked up, catching her eye and giving her a smile that promised heaven. Seconds later, he wedged her legs apart with his, lifted her hips, and plunged inside her. Shock and pleasure hit her at once. She arched and bucked against him, meeting him thrust for thrust.

He pulled her legs around his waist and stared into her eyes. "Deeper," he said, pushing inside her and withdrawing. He did it again. And again. "Take me deeper, Alex. Take both of us deeper."

"Yes," she whispered, and squeezing her legs tight, exploded at his next stroke, shattering into a thousand points of pleasure. Dimly, she heard him say her name, then with one last, powerful lunge, he climaxed deep inside her.

Luke wasn't sure precisely what his plan had been, but he didn't think it had included ravishing Alex. Yet that's exactly what he'd done.

Oh, he'd had every intention of making love to her again, but . . . He turned his head to look at her, but her hair, that dream-inspiring red mane of hers, covered her face. For the first time in his life, he was at a total loss for words. What was he supposed to say to a woman he'd just taken like a madman? Sorry wouldn't quite cover it.

Expecting to see her flinch, he pushed her hair back and gently turned her face up to his. She wore a soft, satisfied, and decidedly smug smile. Relieved, he found himself grinning at her.

He bent down and placed a chaste kiss on her lips. "I don't usually come on like Conan the Barbarian. Did I hurt you?"

"Hmm." It was almost a purr, and the stretch she added to it, more of a sinuous wiggle, carried the feline analogy further. "No. I'm fine."

He wasn't. Poleaxed more accurately described him. He was treading very unfamiliar waters with Alex. And he was pretty sure he didn't like it. Wrapping an arm around her, he settled her against his chest. Neither spoke for a while, and he began to think she'd drifted to sleep.

"Why did you leave the navy?"

Reality crash-landed with her words. His arm tightened around her, then he let her go and sat up against the headboard. "Does it matter?"

Propping herself on her elbow, she studied him. "If I'm going to help you, you're going to have to talk to me."

"Are you going to help me, Alex?"

"Yes." She paused and then covered his hand with her own. "I would have anyway. Even"—she gestured at the bed—"if this hadn't happened."

"That's not why I wanted to make love to you."

"Wasn't it?" she asked quietly. "The truth, Luke."

His original intention had been to get Alex on his side by whatever means necessary. Seducing her to further his cause wasn't something he'd thought of as a hardship. Yet when it had happened, when he actually made love to her, he'd been thinking only of wanting her and finally having her again and nothing at all about any other agenda.

"I won't deny I want your help. But that has nothing to do with my wanting you." She continued to look skeptical. "It was inevitable, Alex, that we'd end up here. I knew it the minute I saw you again. You knew it too."

"Did I? I don't know . . ." she said slowly. "I suppose you're right." Sighing, she rolled onto her back. "None of this is logical," she muttered.

"No, but I'll tell you something that *is* logical. If you expect any talk at all, you'd better put something on. Talking's not going to hold my attention with you stretched out naked in my bed." He rose, crossing to the dresser and pulling a light blue T-shirt out of a drawer.

"I'll get dressed," she said, starting to rise.

"Here, take this." He handed her the shirt. At her raised eyebrow he added, "You might as well. I'm only going to take it off you again later. Unless you've got objections."

She smiled. "No objections."

He pulled on his jeans. "There's a steak in the kitchen calling my name. I'll share if you're hungry."

"Starving."

His shirt looked a lot better on her than it did on him. With her hair tousled and streaming over her shoulders, her lips pouty from his kisses, and the soft cotton barely skimming her legs at mid-thigh, he began to think of other hungers than the one in his belly.

"We need to talk," she said sternly. "Not make love again."

One corner of his mouth lifted. "Reading my mind, Alex?"

"No, just your expression."

He laughed. "All right, you win. We'll talk first."

She waited until he'd slid the steak in the broiler and they were putting together a salad before she brought up the investigation again. But she didn't, as he'd expected, ask him about the navy.

"Let's talk about this idea you have that someone's trying to frame you." She handed him a tomato, which he began to slice.

"It's the only explanation I can think of for why somebody would plant a hundred grand in my bank account."

"I'm not disputing your theory, but we need to explore it further."

He reached across her to pick up a carrot. "Okay, I'm game."

"There are several reasons why a person would try to frame someone else. Sometimes it's simple convenience. If that's the case, then that doesn't give us much of a lead. You are, after all, an obvious suspect."

He slid her a sideways look before he re-sumed slicing vegetables. "Thanks."

"I told you before that anyone connected with the building is suspect." He shrugged and she went on. "But if someone is doing this be-cause they're out to get you, then we have sev-eral avenues to examine."

"Except I can't think of anyone who hates me that much."

"What about your partner? I read about him. About his trial and you testifying against him. And about the firm's problems during and after that. Your partner's indictment for fraud and bribing a public official couldn't have helped your career."

"It destroyed my career," Luke said flatly.

"Then isn't he the obvious choice? You're on your way back up, becoming successful with your new firm, or you were until this hap-pened. Who more likely than a disgruntled partner—"

"Disgruntled *ex*-partner," he corrected her. "But it doesn't matter, Alex. Much as I'd love to blame it on him, and as much as it makes perfect sense, James couldn't have planted that bomb. Or paid someone to either."

"Why not?"

"Because he's dead."

That announcement brought her up short. "Oh. How . . . unfortunate."

Luke couldn't help laughing at the way she

phrased it. He shook his head. "For him, yeah. And for the theory. But it didn't break my heart."

He checked the steak and decided it was ready. A few minutes later, they sat beside each other at his kitchen counter and dug in.

"This is really good," Alex said.

To his amusement, she sounded surprised. "Thanks. Tell me something, why are women always surprised when they find out a man can cook?"

She ate another bite with obvious pleasure. "Because a lot of men can't."

"If they live alone, they usually can."

"You don't know my brother. He thinks cooking is reheating pizza. If it weren't for takeout and delivery, he'd starve to death."

Hearing the affection in her voice, Luke grinned. "Older brother?"

She nodded. "Three years older. Nick's a homicide detective with the same precinct I am."

Luke stopped eating and stared at her. "Nick? As in Nicholas?"

"Please." She raised a hand. "No Russian jokes. I've heard them all."

"Your parents named you Nicholas and Alexandra?"

"Our father has a warped sense of humor."

"Your brother's a cop. I guess that means law enforcement is a family thing with you?"

"Yes. My father was a cop too. Retired now, though. What about you? Was your father navy? Or an architect?"

Deliberately casual, he said, "I never knew him. My mother never talked about him." Which was true—at least until he'd turned fifteen.

"I'm sorry."

Since his parentage was the last thing Luke wanted to discuss, he changed the subject. "So, scratch my ex-partner. Great motive but—"

"Great alibi," Alex finished for him. She speared another bite of steak and chewed thoughtfully. Luke could almost see her mental wheels turning.

"Tell me," she said after a pause, "are you and Waylon Black close?"

"We're friends," he said warily. "Done several projects together."

"And you haven't had any . . . disagreements?"

"Look, Alex, I already told you—"

"Think about it, Luke. I'm asking you to consider the possibility. Waylon Black had the opportunity. Knowledge of the structure that rivals yours. A possible motive, with the insurance money and additional builder's fees. And he knows you."

"Waylon has no grudge against me. Why would he frame me for the crime?"

"Someone has to take the blame. You were

the logical person. I'm not saying he did it, I'm saying it's something to think about. He's a suspect, Luke."

He didn't want to, but he had to consider that she could be right. Had he trusted yet again when he shouldn't have? But Waylon . . . "My gut instincts tell me you're wrong."

"Instincts aren't always dependable," she said harshly. "Facts are."

"You don't have any facts to support this theory either, though, do you? Besides, where would he get the money to put into my account?"

"Stole it."

"He'd have to have some specialized knowledge to do that. Which I'm nearly certain he doesn't have. And why give it to me? If he wanted the money, he could just keep it."

"All right, we'll leave it for now. The investigation is still in the early stages."

He rose and took his dishes to the sink, wishing he could avoid the feeling of déjà vu he was experiencing. Just like James, he thought. No, not quite as bad. At least Waylon hadn't been a boyhood friend of his. His only boyhood friend.

Alex's hand fell on his shoulder and squeezed. "I'm sorry. I know this is hard for you, but I have to look at all the possibilities."

"I understand that." He wished he could

simply take her back to bed, make love to her, and forget the bombing had ever occurred. A glance at her face told him she wasn't through talking. He knew he could sidetrack her for a time, but eventually she'd ask the same questions. And sure enough, she did.

"Tell me about the navy," she said. "Why you joined, and why you quit."

"Come sit down." He walked into the living room and took a seat on the couch, trying to decide how to tell her enough to satisfy her without dredging up a past he preferred to stay buried. She settled beside him, patient and silent.

"I left because the navy—the SEALs—weren't what I'd thought they were. I thought we'd make a difference. I had an idealistic idea of what we were doing, and when reality finally hit me, I got out."

When it had reached the point where he couldn't see much difference between what he was doing and what the enemy was doing, he'd known it was time to go. It was the only thing he could do and still live with himself.

"Black ops?" she asked, her voice gentle.

"The blackest. So clandestine we used to say that even we didn't know what we were doing." His laugh held no humor. "When I'd had as much as I could take, I quit. And"—his mouth curved into a bitter smile—"I haven't blown up anything since then."

"Didn't you consider using the knowledge you'd gained in the SEALs in a civilian career?"

"No." He'd wanted nothing to remind him of his past. Either past.

"Why not? You have a way with explosives."

"Had," he corrected her. It ran in his blood, he thought, still sickened by the memory. That was one thing he wouldn't tell her, and thank God the information was buried where she'd be unlikely to find it.

Alex the woman might believe him, but Senior Corporal Alex Sheridan, the conscientious cop, would have a devil of a time if she knew that he was the son of a man convicted for terrorism.

SEVEN

"When are you going to get an office of your own, kid?" Nick asked, strolling up to Alex's desk.

"Judgment Day," she mumbled without looking up from her work.

Nick's hand appeared in front of her eyes, flourishing something. "I've got two tickets to the Ranger game tonight. How about it?"

Her attention snared, Alex cocked her head to look up at him. "What happened to Bambi?"

"Bunny."

"Whatever." She waved a hand. "Your latest true love."

"She dumped me. Swear to God, I stand before you a heartbroken man." He laid his hand over his heart and sighed deeply.

Alex thought she'd never seen anyone less

heartbroken than her brother just then, and said so. "Why did she dump you?"

"Well . . ." He took a chair, turned it around, and straddled it. "I forgot her birthday. Went out with the guys instead of meeting her for dinner."

"You did it on purpose," Alex said, knowing her brother.

"Alex." He looked pained. "It was dinner with her folks. Hell, I could practically hear her humming the 'Wedding March.' There's no way I could do it."

"You're a pig, Nick."

"But you love me anyway," he said, and grinned. "Are you still on that latest bombing case? What did you end up doing about your problem?"

Slept with him, she thought, and complicated matters even more. "I'm still working it out," she said evasively. She had spent all morning trying to find a motive for Waylon Black and had come up with zip. According to what she'd discovered, he was exactly what he appeared to be. A hardworking, honest builder with no large debts or gambling problems or anything that might imply he needed fast money.

And nothing to suggest he hated Luke enough to frame him for the crime.

She could tell by his expression that Nick wasn't about to let it go at that. Luckily, her phone rang, which at least delayed his interrogation. Thankfully, she snatched it up. "Alex Sheridan."

"When can my team inspect the damaged wing?"

Luke, she thought. Both amused and annoyed, she asked, "Do you always start conversations this abruptly?"

"Yeah. I hate the phone. So when are you going to let us in?"

"Possibly this afternoon, but more likely tomorrow." She smiled, hearing his impatient curse. "I'm sorry, I know you're anxious to get started." Mouthing a thanks at the sergeant who'd just handed her a file, she laid it on her desk.

"Not just me," Luke was saying. "Alsobrook's been foaming at the mouth to know the extent of the damage. I'll arrange for my team to meet there first thing in the morning unless you tell me otherwise."

"That sounds like the best plan."

"Alex." He hesitated a moment before he continued. "I've been thinking over what you said and decided you're right. I have to consider Waylon a suspect."

Aware of her brother's razor-sharp gaze on her, Alex turned her chair so that her back was toward him. If she thought Nick would listen to her, she'd tell him to leave, but an intimate knowledge of his nature told her that would be futile. He'd leave when he was good and ready and not a minute before.

Lowering her voice, she said, "I know you don't want to believe it, but it's the obvious answer."

"I'm considering it, but I'm not convinced yet. But with that in mind, I've been looking through the construction orders. So far I haven't found anything out of the ordinary."

"You have access to all of them?"

"As the liaison between the contractor and the owner, I'm privy to all orders for materials as well as the labor charges. All the bills pertaining to the construction of the project are routed through me. Thought you might want to see them."

"Absolutely. Saves me having to get a court order. You're at your office?"

"Yeah. You'll come yourself, won't you?"

She smiled, for though he'd phrased it as a question, it had sounded more like an order. Clearly, Luke was a man accustomed to being in charge. "Definitely. Is that all?"

"Not by a long shot. Will I see you tonight?"

Her heart leaped, her pulse quickening at the thought. "I'm not sure how late I'll be."

"I'll wait. I'd like to take you to dinner."

She'd love to go to dinner with him, but she didn't think her being seen with one of the suspects in a social setting would be such a great idea. "Better not."

"Ashamed of me, Alex?"

She wondered if she imagined the hurt behind the amusement in his tone. "You know that's not it."

"Will you come to my place, then? Or let me come to yours?" His voice deepened, sending a shiver of sensual awareness up her spine. "I want to be with you tonight."

Alex tried to control the giddy rush that his words sent singing through her bloodstream. "I'd like that too," she said softly.

"Good. I'll see you in a little while, then."

She hung up and turned to face her brother. One look at his expression warned her he was after answers. Noticing he held her newest file in his hands and had been leafing through it, she took the offensive.

"Get your hands off my stuff. This isn't a homicide investigation. You don't need to look at that."

Typically, he ignored her. "That was the problem, I take it? Now, how did you put it? Oh, yeah, I remember. The suspect you're not *exactly* involved with."

Alex thrust her chin up and glared at her brother. "Who says I'm involved now?"

He dismissed her response with a vulgar word. "Your voice sounded like melted butter when you were talking just now. I've never heard you sound like that in your life. What's going on with you? You're not acting like yourself."

Nick was right, she thought. She hadn't been herself since she'd tumbled into bed with Luke Morgan the night she met him. But she'd never known anyone like Luke before. Never been . . . Reeling, she rested her forehead on her hand. Good God, she wasn't in love with him. Couldn't possibly be. It was absurd to think she could have fallen in love with a man in the space of days.

It hit her hard, stealing her breath, landing like a blow in the middle of her chest. She hadn't fallen in love in the space of days. She'd fallen in love with Luke Morgan in one night.

One reckless night three weeks before.

"Well, well." She heard Nick's voice as if from a distance. "Your problem suspect wouldn't happen to be an explosives expert, would he?"

She shook her head hard to try to clear her mind. "What? What are you talking about?"

"According to this"—he waved a piece of paper, then read aloud from it—" 'expert knowledge of both explosives and structural placement of charges indicated.' " He raised his head and met her gaze. "A pro set the charge that blew up the Alsobrook building."

A pro, she thought, her head spinning. A professional.

An ex-navy SEAL?

Half an hour later Alex stood in Luke's outer office, trying unsuccessfully to defend herself against an irate woman half her size and twenty years her senior.

Eyes flashing, hands on her hips, she stood between Alex and Luke's office door as if she were his bodyguard and Alex the assassin out to get him. "If you think for one minute that Luke blew up that building, then you're crazier than a hound dog on lithium, is all I've got to say."

She'd said that and a good deal more in the few minutes Alex had been there. "Look, Miss—" Alex began.

"Kathy Harper." Folding her arms across her chest, she tapped her foot menacingly. "I've worked for Luke Morgan for almost two years and I'm telling you right now you're barking up the wrong tree."

Wondering if she always spoke in dog analogies, Alex attempted to soothe her. "Your loyalty is commendable. However, at the moment, Mr. Morgan hasn't been singled out as a suspect."

"I heard him talking to Waylon Black and I

know you think he might have done it. I'm just telling you, he didn't. Why, the very—"

"Kathy, I think Detective Sheridan gets the picture," Luke said from his office doorway. "And she's here at my request."

Far from being repentant, the secretary merely snorted and returned to her desk without giving Alex so much as a sideways glance.

"Wow," Alex said in his office a moment later. "I had no idea you inspired so much loyalty."

"Surprised me a little too," he said, shutting the door. "For one thing I didn't know she'd heard Waylon and me talking, but when Waylon's mad he doesn't talk, he shouts."

He took a step toward her, but she held up her hand to ward him off. "Don't come any nearer. I'm working."

Amusement warmed his eyes as he halted a few steps away. "I wasn't planning to seduce you in my office, Alex."

"Maybe not, but you looked like you were about to kiss me."

He nodded, smiling. "Perceptive. It seemed like a good idea to me."

"It's not." Agitated, she took a turn around the room. "We have important things to talk about and when we—it's just not a good idea." She couldn't afford to be any more distracted than she already was.

He leaned back against his desk. "Okay, if

that's the way you want it. What's so important?"

"We have reason to believe that a professional set the charge."

His expression sobered. "Why?"

"I can't tell you that. I'm already out on a limb telling you anything at all."

"Don't you think my engineering team will come to the same conclusion?"

"Probably, though I don't know how long it will take them to figure it out. But that's not the point. Do you understand what I'm saying, Luke?"

"Yeah. A pro set the charges. So?"

"So?" Exasperated, she glared at him. "So it doesn't look good for you. In fact, it looks terrible for you."

"No more so than it already did."

"There are plenty of professionals around, willing to do any job for the right price," she said, starting to pace. "But the fact remains that you're a professional too."

"Ex-professional," he reminded her. "Alex, I haven't had anything to do with explosives in years. Not since I left the SEALs. Haven't so much as touched a blasting cap."

"I believe you, of course, but—"

"Do you?" he interrupted.

She stopped pacing and frowned at him. "If I didn't, I wouldn't be here. Would I be warning you if I really thought you'd done it?"

"You don't have any doubts at all."

"No," she said, but she didn't meet his eyes. She believed him. It was just that sometimes she worried that she might be too involved to think rationally about him. She hurried on before he could speak again. "This strengthens your case that the bomber is someone who's out to get you. Someone who knows you. Who would know about your military service? It's not that easy to get that information."

"Waylon does, but there's another problem. He's no professional. He knows nothing about demolitions. Couldn't set off a firecracker without burning his fingers."

"He knows the structure, though, doesn't he? He's the general contractor, he's bound to."

"Yeah." He frowned. "Waylon is as familiar with it as I am. Almost."

"Maybe he's working with someone. And that person is the one who's trying to frame you."

"But why bring in Waylon? If the guy's a pro, he wouldn't need Waylon's knowledge of the structure. All he'd have to do is get hold of the blueprints."

She tapped her fingers on her arm. "You have a point," she conceded. "Though he might have used Waylon to get the blueprints. But I still want those construction orders."

He picked up a thick file folder from his

desk and handed it to her. "These are the copies. I've kept the originals in my files."

"Thanks. I'll start on these as soon as I get back." She tucked the folder under her arm. "Okay, let's take another track. Did you make any enemies when you were in the navy?"

"Not that I'm aware of. Even when I left . . ." He shook his head. "No, my team wasn't the problem. The problems I had were with the navy itself. My team members understood where I was coming from. At least, I thought they did. Besides, why would they wait this long to come after me? I've been out of the service for years now."

"It's still something else to check out. I'll need the names of your team members. And anyone else you had contact with."

"Alex, I think you're reaching here."

She met his gaze levelly. "No, I'm not. In fact, it makes perfect sense. Your fellow team members not only know about your military service, they had demolitions training as well. Perfect setup."

He still looked skeptical but told her he'd call her with the names later that day.

"Good. I'll put someone on it as soon as I get them." She headed for the door, saying, "I need to get back to the station."

"Hold on a minute." Luke walked over and stood in front of her, smiling down at her in a way that made her heart rate speed up and the blood heat in her veins. Irritation flashed through her that he should have that kind of effect on her with a simple look.

Before she could speak, he cupped her face, tilted her head back, and murmured, "Something to remind you not to work too late," just before his mouth covered hers.

Slow, hot, thorough, he took his time kissing her until her breasts started to ache, her knees threatened to buckle, and her mind—what was left of it—had gone numb.

"Until tonight," he said in that deep, seductive voice that made her skin tingle and her bones turn to jelly.

Afraid she'd babble if she tried to speak, Alex left without another word.

EIGHT

Luke didn't like waiting, and he especially didn't like waiting for a woman. In fact, he couldn't remember ever doing so before. Here he was, though, hanging around Alex's apartment complex, waiting for her to get home.

He'd found himself doing a lot of things lately that he'd never done before, and they were all related to Alex Sheridan. For instance, he'd been forced to trust her. It wasn't so much that he didn't place a lot of faith in women, but he didn't like having to rely on anyone. The last person he'd trusted to any degree was Waylon and it was beginning to look like that had been a mistake.

But Alex Sheridan was all that stood between him and a charge of terrorism.

If that wasn't disturbing enough, he reflected, he had a bad feeling that he was obsessed with Alex the woman, aside from needing Alex the cop. Making love with her the night before hadn't assuaged his desire in the least. He didn't hold much hope that tonight would leave him feeling any different.

He should be happy, he supposed, that she'd given him her address when he'd called her earlier with the information she'd wanted about his SEAL team. Apparently, her address and phone number were closely guarded secrets, which made sense, considering her profession.

Alex drove up just then and got out of her car, affording him an inspiring view of her long, enticing legs as she leaned back inside to get something. A surge of lust hit him, tempting him to find out her opinion of fast, hot sex in cramped quarters, but he restrained himself. He could wait until they got to her apartment. Maybe.

Just as he reached her she turned around. Startled, she swore at him.

"Dammit, Luke! Don't sneak up on me like that! You're lucky I didn't maim you first and ask questions later. My God, do you have any idea how many women are accosted in parking lots daily?"

"Sorry." He couldn't help grinning. "Do you think you could?"

"Maim you?" She flashed him a wicked smile. "You bet. I'm a cop, remember?"

Taking her briefcase in one hand and her arm in the other, Luke walked with her to her apartment. The architect in him wondered if the developers had pulled a blueprint from Apartments "R" Us when they built the place. One of the dozens of complexes in this section of North Dallas apartments row, it was as nondescript as any he'd seen.

"How do you tell which one is yours?" he asked. "They all look alike."

"Safety in anonymity," she said over her shoulder as she opened the door. "I like it that way."

They didn't get two steps inside her apartment before he had her backed up against the door with his hands beneath her skirt and her fingers grappling with his shirt buttons.

"Luke," she said between openmouthed kisses. "Doesn't this"—she moaned and threw back her head as he nipped her throat— "doesn't this worry you?"

"What?" he asked, sliding his hands over her sweet little rear and pressing her against him. The only thing he was worried about was lasting long enough to get inside her.

"That we"—she groaned when he dipped his hands beneath her hose and panties to find bare skin—"want each other like this? So much?"

"Not at the moment." He stroked her where she was hot and wet and waiting for him. "Right now the only thing I'm thinking about is being inside you."

She took his face in her hands and gazed into his eyes. "I want you," she said, and there was no more talk.

"Nice apartment," Luke said sometime later, glancing around her living room. Sort of a traditional-modern style, he thought, admiring it. A white camel-backed couch was set in front of the window, flanked by jade-green leather Parson chairs. The top of the light-colored oak coffee table was partially obscured by a couple of art books and a book on criminal codes. A paperback science-fiction novel lay open on the couch.

Alex came out of the kitchen carrying two glasses of wine. "I thought you said they all looked alike?"

"Not on the inside. It suits you." He looked around, trying to put a name to it. "It's classy." He squinted at a large impressionist painting hanging over a pine French Provincial sideboard. "That's not a Monet, is it?"

She laughed and handed him a glass. "I wish. No, I found it at a flea market, believe it or not. It's amazing some of the things you can find if you're persistent."

"Thanks," he said, taking the glass from her. He sipped his wine and, intrigued by the photos along her mantel, walked over for a closer look. Framed snapshots as well as more formal poses were spread over the beautifully carved wood. Luke picked up a snapshot of a tall, dark-haired man smiling at the camera, his arm draped across Alex's shoulders. He didn't at all like the sting of what he recognized as jealousy.

She crossed the room to stand beside him. Her silky robe, a deep blue just like her eyes, shifted open as she walked, giving him tantalizing glimpses of her bare legs. He had an idea that creamy skin was the only thing she was wearing beneath it. And though it hadn't been long since they'd made love, he was tempted to find out for sure right then and there.

"That's my brother." She sounded amused, making him wonder what his expression had been.

"The homicide detective." He didn't care for the relief her words brought him either. "You don't look a lot alike. Maybe in the eyes, but that's it."

She nodded. "Nick likes to say he got the beauty and I got the brains."

Luke smiled at her. "He needs a pair of glasses, then. I'd say you got both."

Her mouth kicked up at the corners. "But then you're not female."

"No, and I'm not your brother either, thank God."

She laughed and sipped her wine, then pointed out some other pictures. "These are my parents," she said of an older couple in front of a mobile home. "When my dad retired they bought the fanciest mobile home they could afford and now they're working their way through the states."

His gaze caught on a photo of Alex and a blonde woman, both dressed in some kind of protective gear. Bomb suits? he wondered. "I didn't realize you were qualified in bomb disposal."

"Everyone in the unit is. We have to get recertified every year. I worked bomb disposal for several years before becoming an investigator." Picking up the photo, she ran her thumb over the two young faces. After a pause she said, "Jenna was my partner."

Jenna. The name she'd cried out that night in San Diego. "Was?"

Her face expressionless, her eyes blank, she glanced at him. "She died."

"I'm sorry."

"It's a risky occupation." She shrugged and turned away. "We all know that when we join the unit."

He set his glass on the mantel. "But you still have nightmares about it." And still wanted to forget, he thought.

She whirled around to face him. "How did you . . . ?"

"The night we spent together in San Diego. You called out her name."

"You . . ." She stopped and cleared her throat. "You remember that?"

He took her glass and set it beside his. "I remember everything about that night, Alex." He touched her cheek, slid his hand down to caress her throat. "What we said." His hand lingered on the soft skin, and he could feel her pulse flutter. "What we did." He kissed her neck, lowering his hand to cup her breast, and smiled at her hiss of indrawn breath. His voice grew husky. "What it felt like to be inside you the first time." He took her lips, kissed her deeply. "And the next," he murmured against her mouth.

She sighed. "If you're trying to seduce me, it's working."

Her belt came loose with a tug, and he slipped her robe from her shoulders, sliding it down her arms until it pooled at her feet. Just as he'd imagined, she was naked. And beautiful. He swung her up in his arms and carried her to the bedroom.

It wasn't until much later, until after he'd poured himself into her and she'd taken him like she'd never get enough, convulsing so sweetly and completely around him, that the realization dawned on him.

He knew why he was obsessed with her, with making love to her. Knew why he wanted to know everything about her, why he felt a driving urge to assuage the pain he sometimes saw in her eyes. Why he wanted her to believe in him. Why he'd been so angry when she left him and why he'd been so damned determined to have her again no matter what he had to do.

He was in love with her.

At least now he knew why he hadn't been able to forget her. He cradled her damp body against his own while their breathing slowed, their heartbeats steadied. Her fingers traced lazy patterns on his back while he ran his hand from her silky hair down to the curve of her hips and back up again.

After a time, he rolled away from her, then pulled her into his arms, her back to his chest, and planted a kiss on the side of her neck.

"Tell me about Jenna," he said.

Jenna, Alex thought. Why was he bringing her up now? When he'd left it alone earlier, had made love to her instead, she'd thought he understood. Pushing away from him, she lay on her back and stared at the ceiling. "You sure know how to ruin a mood."

"Talk to me, Alex." He took one of her hands and raised it to his lips to kiss it.

She turned to look at him. "Why?"

"Because you need to."

"Don't you think I've talked about it before? I've been to the police shrink. They make you do that when you lose a partner."

"I don't care who you've talked to, you haven't resolved it. You wouldn't be having recurrent nightmares if you had."

"One nightmare in the last year isn't recurring."

"And that's all you've had." He sounded skeptical.

"That's what I said, isn't it?" she snapped.

"So you're saying you've resolved it. You're okay about it."

She jerked her hand from his and sat up. "Hell, no, I'm not okay. I'll never resolve Jenna's death. But I'm living with it. I have no choice. How can you deal with being responsible for your partner's death?"

"Is that what happened? Are you responsible?"

"Yes." She leaned back against the headboard, silent, waiting for him to press her, but he didn't. He knew exactly how to play her, she thought, waiting so patiently for her to break down and talk to him. And, of course, she did.

She closed her eyes, then opened them, still seeing the scene that haunted her. "I dream about her. About her death. And every time I dream it, I know I could have stopped her. Should have stopped her. Jenna wasn't ready. It should have been me, not her."

He was sitting up, too, understanding in his

gaze as he watched her. "Then you'd be dead instead of her. Is that what you want?"

She shook her head violently. "No, I wouldn't be. Or I might not be. When I saw her reach for that door, I—I had this feeling. I knew what was going to happen, knew something was wrong. Terribly wrong. And then . . . The car exploded the instant she touched the right-rear-door handle."

"Your partner was doing her job. She was trained, wasn't she?"

"Oh, yes, she was trained." Her fists twisted in the sheets. "But she wasn't ready and I knew it."

"You believe you should have trusted your instincts."

"No. That's just it." Passing a hand over her brow, she grimaced, wishing she could explain it better. To him, and to herself. "I don't know if I'd have had the same gut feeling if it had been me. And now, I'll never know. Instincts . . . I don't trust them anymore."

"You're trusting me. And you don't have much to go on besides instinct. All the facts—"

"Are circumstantial evidence. Not good enough to convict you, even if I believed you'd done it." And she couldn't, wouldn't believe he had. But she was relying on facts, not instinct.

The fact that she couldn't possibly have fallen in love with the kind of man who would bomb a building.

NINE

The SEAL-team lead Alex had held such hopes for was beginning to look like another dead end. Sifting through the information she'd collected earlier that morning, she snorted in disgust. Two of the team's six members were dead, two others were still in the navy on a clandestine assignment, and one of them was Luke. That left one, and Alex hadn't been able to locate him.

Her efforts to discover anything about the electronic transfer into Luke's account had been spectacularly unsuccessful as well. And the person assigned to check out Alsobrook had found nothing to indicate he could be behind the bombing. However, there was still a possibility that one of the construction workers who had a beef with Waylon Black or Alsobrook had done it.

Taken as a whole, though, she didn't have squat.

A clerk came by and dropped a bundle of mail on her desk. Alex groaned and reached for it, thinking she might as well handle it now instead of piling it on top of the massive heap of correspondence already awaiting her attention. Most of it was easily dealt with, and she was nearly through when she opened an envelope with no return address. She laid the envelope aside in case it contained something of interest.

Pulling out a microfiche copy of a newspaper clipping with a piece of paper stapled behind it, she spread it out on her desk. The photo caught her eye, and picking it up, she inspected the picture more closely. Luke? she wondered, frowning. In handcuffs? No, not Luke, she realized the longer she gazed at it. But the man in the photo looked enough like him to be his brother.

As she began reading she realized that the paper was dated twenty-one years earlier. The caption beneath the picture read: *Dixon Banks, convicted on charges of terrorism and mass murder in the bombing of a St. Louis, Missouri, post office earlier this year.*

Her heart started to pound, her stomach tightened, even before she turned the page to see what was behind the clipping. Another photocopy, this time of a birth certificate. The birth certificate of a baby boy named Lucas Morgan, born to Marie Morgan Banks and Dixon Edward Banks.

Not his brother. His father.

Luke's father was a convicted terrorist.

Her stomach rolled and clenched as the realization sank in. The sick feeling gradually subsided and her blood began to heat. With a vicious curse, she slammed the papers down on the desk. She'd risked her career, and worse, her heart, and Luke had done nothing but lie to her. Alex wasn't sure whether she was angrier at herself for trusting him, or at him for keeping something so important from her.

One more piece of circumstantial evidence that made Luke Morgan look guilty as sin.

Tracking Luke down wasn't hard. Alex drove to the Alsobrook site at quitting time that afternoon. What she had to say to him wasn't for spectators, so she had waited to go until she was certain most of the workers would have left for the day.

She knew better than to be alone with him at one of their apartments. Even as angry as she was, she recognized her complete lack of will-power where he was concerned. He'd talk and soothe all her doubts and questions in no time, and before she realized it, she'd be right back in bed with him. Not this time, she thought. This time she intended to keep the upper hand.

He was standing beside his car smiling at her when she drove up and took the space next to his. Her heartbeat quickened at the sight of him, infuriating her still further. He looked good, as he always did. Today he wore jeans and a faded red T-shirt in deference to the mess she knew he'd been crawling around in.

She got out of her car and slammed the door shut. "I need to see you privately. Now." Not waiting for his answer, she turned her back and stalked to the temporary building that was Waylon Black's office.

"Nice to see you too," he said, catching up to her in a couple of strides.

She shot him a furious glance. "I'm not in the mood for small talk."

One of his eyebrows rose and an ironic smile curved his mouth. "Or civility?"

"That either," she snapped, waiting for him to unlock the door and then striding inside when he did so.

"Should I stand or sit while you take my head off?" He sounded amused.

She wondered how amused he'd be when she dropped her little bombshell on him. Ignoring his provocative comment, she withdrew a file from her briefcase and threw it down on the desk. "Take a look at this."

He reached down, flipped open the manila

folder, and stood silently looking at the article. Beyond an almost imperceptible thinning of his lips, he showed no reaction.

She waited a moment and, when he didn't speak, said, "Look behind the clipping."

He lifted the clipping to see the photocopied birth certificate behind it. His jaw muscles tightened, but that was the only betraying action he made. Letting the paper fall, he shut the folder and looked at her, his eyes a flat, lifeless gray.

"So?"

She wanted to choke him. How could he possibly stand there so calmly, so damned unemotional? She flicked the folder back open, jabbing a finger at the photo. "Are you going to deny this man is your father?"

"No."

That single, abrupt syllable fanned her already flaming wrath to wildfire proportions. "Did it just slip your mind that your father"— she slammed her hand down on the picture— "your *father*, for God's sake, is a terrorist? Or didn't you think it was important enough to tell me?"

Luke folded his arms across his chest and leaned back against the desk. "No."

If she were a man, Alex thought, she'd slug him. Not only was he in deep trouble, but her career was on the line and he didn't seem to have a clue. Or care, either. "No, it didn't slip your mind, or no, you didn't think it was important?" she forced herself to ask calmly.

He shrugged. "That's my father, not me. He's dead, by the way. Died in prison."

"I know, I looked him up. Luke, why the hell didn't you tell me this? Why did you keep it quiet? Don't you understand how this looks?"

"I'm sure you'll tell me."

"I'd like to hit you," she said through her teeth. "And if you don't stop being so—" She broke off, aware that giving in to her anger wouldn't help either of them. But what was wrong with him?

"This is just one more layer in the case that's being built against you. Don't act like you don't realize that. Couldn't you have trusted me enough to tell me?" Pain invaded alongside the anger. "After—after what's happened between us, you didn't feel you could trust me?"

"It has nothing to do with trust. My father—whatever he was, whatever he did—has no bearing on the case." His voice was flat, unemotional, as uninterested as if he were discussing the weather.

He was still leaning against the desk, looking at her in the same dispassionate way, his thoughts and emotions reined in so tightly, it would take an explosion to loosen them. She was mad enough to oblige him.

"Ordinarily, I'd agree with you," she said, "but in this case, I'm afraid it does have bearing. Now, are you going to tell me about it? About him?"

He shoved himself away from the desk and walked to the door. "No, I'm not."

Stupefied, she stared at him. "Don't you dare leave. We're not finished here."

"I am," he said, and walked out.

For about thirty seconds, she stood there with her mouth hanging open, then she ran to the door and wrenched it open. She started to call after him, but other than cussing him out, she couldn't think of anything to say. Besides, he wasn't listening. Nothing she said would get through to him, anyway.

Her eyebrows raised as she watched him get in his car and peel out in a thick cloud of gravel and dust. Judging by his driving, he wasn't nearly as calm as he'd appeared. Unnaturally calm.

Something was very wrong here and she didn't think it had anything to do with the bombing of the Alsobrook building.

God, how classic that his past should surface again now, at the moment it could do him the most harm, Luke thought. He cursed as he shifted into fourth. *My father, the terrorist. Thanks, Dad.*

His hands gripped the steering wheel tightly as the traffic swirled around him in an unfocused blur of motion. He'd thought he had a handle on all the old feelings, but the sight of that newspaper article had slammed into his mind and soul like a knockout punch, the violent, churning nausea as strong as it had been when he saw the picture for the first time and heard the truth about his parentage.

"See that, boy? That there's your old man," his stepfather had taunted. *"See what kind of blood you spring from? The devil's in your blood, boy, and you're gonna end up just like your daddy."*

Just like your daddy.

In that instant, he'd known why his stepfather had always hated him.

But he wasn't a fifteen-year-old kid any longer. And this time he stood to lose more than an abusive home life with an indifferent mother and a stepfather who made his life a living hell. This time he would lose his freedom.

And Alex.

Alex, he thought, downshifting as the traffic slowed. How the hell had she found out about his father? The information wasn't impossible to find, particularly for a cop, but she'd have needed a reason to search for it. No ordinary background check would have turned up his birth certificate. She would have had to know where to start looking, and she shouldn't have had any idea.

What had sent her searching into his past?

Around one A.M. Luke was pounding on Alex's apartment door.

Several hours spent in a bar wishing for a good fight hadn't taken his mind off his problems, especially since no one had come near him except the bartender and a woman he'd driven off with a snarl. Unable to get drunk either, he'd gone home, only to find that sleep was a joke. Finally, he gave up trying and decided to confront Alex.

But he'd be damned if he was going to tell her anything. No, she was going to tell him where—and why—she'd dug up his family history.

He slammed his fist against her door again, not caring if he woke every neighbor she had. "It's Luke. Open up." He heard her voice, muffled and cursing him as she grappled with the chain and swung the door open.

"What the hell do you think you're doing showing up here at this time of night?" Her hair was tousled, her voice hoarse from sleep, but her eyes were wide-awake and blazingly angry.

She fell back a step when he shoved her aside and walked in. He didn't blame her. He had an idea he looked pretty raw and he damned well knew he felt like bloody meat.

"You're drunk," she said, pulling her pale blue robe tight around her. "I can smell it from here."

"No, I'm not. But I'd sure as hell like to be," he said, stalking the room, anger fueling his footsteps.

"There's the door." She waved a hand at it. "Don't let me stop you."

He ignored that in favor of scowling at her. "What made you look for it? Why were you digging around in my past? You had no reason—"

"I had every reason," she interrupted, her voice icy calm in direct contrast to his own. "And every right. I'm investigating this case. It's my job to look into anything I think might hold a clue as to who bombed the Alsobrook building."

"So you went looking for all the sordid facts you could find."

She parked a hand on her hip and surveyed him coolly. "As it happens, I wasn't looking for anything. Someone sent it to me."

He halted, staring at her. In three strides he reached her side and grasped her arms. "What? You mean you didn't—"

"It came in the mail." Her gaze fell to his hands on her arms, then raised back up to his face. "Now let go of me before you have to crawl out of here."

It wasn't an idle bluff, he knew. Realizing he'd been gripping her arms tight enough to leave bruises, he dropped his hands. She probably thought he'd lost it, and she wouldn't be far wrong. "Who sent it?"

"It came anonymously." Her gaze raked him sardonically. "What did you think?"

He shoved his hands through his hair, trying to make sense of what she had just told him. "There wasn't anything to identify where it came from?"

"Nothing except a local postmark. No fingerprints, no identifying marks. Nothing."

His mind didn't want to function. He sank onto her couch, his head dropping into his hands. "Dammit, this doesn't make sense."

"Of course it does," she said impatiently. "Who knows about this? Does Waylon Black?"

"No. No one knows."

"Obviously, someone does. Someone sent me that clipping and birth certificate."

He raised his head and met her gaze directly. "The only people who knew, who would even know where to start looking for material like this, are dead."

"All of them?"

"All of them. My mother, my stepfather. James. Every stinking one of—"

The thought hit him with a chill blast.

No, it couldn't be. James was dead, his body lost somewhere amid the 747 plane wreckage off Florida's Gulf Coast. Unmourned, unmarked.

He stared at Alex, knowing it was insane. Knowing it was true.

"The son of a bitch is alive."

TEN

"Who's alive?" Alex asked sharply. Luke continued to stare at her as if a live charge had just gone off in his mind. "What are you talking about?"

"James," he said finally. "He's alive. It's so bloody perfect. I can't believe I didn't realize it before."

He'd denied being drunk, she thought, but he wasn't quite sober either. "When I asked you the first time if it could have been your partner—"

"I know, I said he was dead. And I believed it . . . then. But what if he isn't?"

Her eyebrows drew together in a frown. "Luke, I think you need to sleep on this—"

He sprang up from the couch and grabbed hold of her arms again. "Dammit, Alex, I'm not drunk!"

His touch was gentler this time, but she could see the riot of emotions simmering in his eyes. Pain and fury were among them, as well as a sharp edge of determination. And though she could tell he'd been drinking, she admitted he didn't look bombed by any means.

"All right, you're not drunk. Then what are you saying?"

"James reportedly died in an airplane crash off the Florida coast. But get this." His gaze bored into hers, his fingers tightening on her arms. "His body was never recovered."

It sounded fantastic, but . . . She shook her head, trying to gather her thoughts. "Tell me the date of the plane crash and I'll check into it."

"I don't know the exact date, but it was in all the papers. About a year ago, August. Mid-August, I think. A big jet went down off the Florida Gulf Coast."

"You're certain no body was recovered?"

He dropped his hands and made an impatient gesture. "According to all reports, three bodies were never found. James Bennett's was one of them."

Pinned by his intense gaze, she conceded the possibility. "It's worth checking into, at the least."

"It's perfect," he repeated. He laughed sharply, though with no humor. "Exactly what he'd do. James was always a quick thinker.

That plane crash must have seemed like a sign from heaven to him. He'd been given some time to put his affairs in order before he started serving his term and that's when it happened. He must have used the mess that followed the plane's crash to disappear. With the chaos of the accident scene, nothing would have been easier. And he's been waiting ever since for payback."

"Why? Why would he go to all this trouble? Because you testified against him at his trial?"

He glanced at her, then looked away. "More or less. It's a long story."

"I'm not going anywhere," she said, and took a seat on the couch. She was tired, exhausted from lack of sleep and stress, but this was a story she intended to hear. "You're the one who came to me in the middle of the night. Now I think it's time you gave me some answers."

He looked down at her, hesitating, and she added, "And not only about your ex-partner. I want some answers about your father, too, and I don't give a rat's damn if you don't want to talk about it."

"You don't ask for much, do you?" he asked wearily.

"I think the fact that I've put my career on the line for you entitles me to the truth. What do you think?"

He closed his eyes and muttered a curse. She could see him clenching his jaw, knew he was still struggling. Trying to decide just how much to tell her? she wondered.

"All right," he said finally. "You're right, I owe you." Sitting beside her on the couch, he propped his forearms on his thighs, linked his fingers together, and stared down at the floor. He was silent for several minutes.

"Three people knew about my father," he said at length. "My mother and stepfather are both dead. I know that for certain. That leaves James."

"Other people could have found out."

He shook his head. "Not very easily. It would be damned hard to find unless you knew where to look. A private detective could find the information, eventually, and so could the police or the FBI. But anyone else would need to know where to look to get those papers that were mailed to you. And James would have known exactly where to find them."

"Does Bennett hate you enough to do this? Bomb a building and frame you for it?"

"Yeah." He gave a caustic laugh. "My testimony convicted him. He never figured I'd do it. Because of our past, and because he'd helped me get started in architecture in the first place, he thought I'd look the other way. But I didn't. When he realized he had me figured wrong, he saw it as a betrayal. The last thing he said to me was that he'd get even. He picked a poetic revenge, I'll say that for him."

"Why did he believe you wouldn't testify against him? He must have had a reason to think that."

His arms still propped on his thighs, his hands clenched together, he said heavily, "Because I owed him."

"For getting you started in your career?"

"Partly." He shook his head again and looked at her. "But there's a lot more to it. I've owed him since I was fifteen years old. If it hadn't been for James, and for his mother and father, I'd be dead."

The way he said it, so simply and matter-of-factly, she didn't think he was exaggerating. She remained silent, letting him unfold the story.

When he began speaking again, his voice was devoid of expression. A recitation of facts with his emotions left out. "I never knew much about my past. Never knew my father at all. I knew my mother married young and divorced him when I was two. Both of us went by her maiden name. I never had a birth certificate. She told the schools that the courthouse had burned. She never spoke about my father, never told me anything about him. Whenever I asked, she shut me up with the back of her hand, so I quit asking. Either she had no family or she'd cut her ties with them because I never met any of them.

"My mother tolerated me all right until I got older. But the older I got, and I found out later, the more I looked like my old man, the less she liked me. My mouth—I was a real smart-ass as a teenager—didn't help, either. Then, when I was about thirteen, she married again."

His tone hadn't changed, he was still speaking quietly with no emotion coloring his voice, but Alex could see his hands clenching into fists, could sense the tension within him, ready to erupt.

"Things went downhill in a hurry after that. Bart, her husband, hated my guts, but I didn't know why until I was fifteen."

"Did he . . ." Afraid she knew the answer, she hesitated before she finished. "Did he abuse you?"

Luke gave her a sardonic glance and nodded. "Beat the hell out of me regularly. Said he'd beat the devil out of me"—he grinned quickly, bitterly—"but I got too big for him to take on before he managed to do it."

"Did your mother know?"

His shoulder lifted in a careless shrug. "Yeah. I don't think she knew how bad it was, but she knew he smacked me around."

And obviously hadn't stopped it, Alex

thought, aching for the child he'd been, furious at the woman who'd called herself a mother.

"James was my best friend," he went on. "One of my only ones, as a matter of fact. He had his license, and we used to go cruising. You know, drink a little beer, pick up some chicks. Or try to." He smiled briefly before his face grew grim again. "One night James decided to stay at my place because he was afraid his old man would find out he'd been drinking. It was easier to sneak in at my place. Except that night it wasn't. When we got in, old Bart was laying for me."

His voice had changed now. It held pain and a cold anger she could feel as well as hear.

"God knows why my mother had told him about my old man, but she had. He had a newspaper article about the bombing all laid out for me to see. I'm sure he enjoyed it even more with James there to hear the story. So he told me the truth. That my father had been charged with terrorism and mass murder. I called him a lying bastard and he showed me my birth certificate. The one my mother swore she didn't have. The one she said had burned in a courthouse fire. I wish to God it had."

Alex closed her eyes, drawing in a deep breath. Fifteen years old, she thought. So young to have his life fall apart. "What happened then?"

His eyes were hooded, dark with an old anger that had never died and she doubted ever would. "I went for his throat, which was just what he'd been waiting for. We had a hell of a fight. James tried to stop us, but all he got out of it was a bloody nose."

His stepfather was dead, he'd said. But he hadn't said when he died. An involuntary gasp escaped her as she considered the possibility. Had Luke . . . ? No, she didn't believe he could have killed the man, no matter what he'd been feeling. Every instinct told her Luke was no killer.

Something of what she'd been thinking must have shown on her face because he said harshly, "No, I didn't kill him. The shape I was in, I was no match for him."

"I didn't think you had."

"Didn't you?"

"No, I didn't." She shook her head and touched his arm, wanting to comfort.

He shook her off and stood, pacing away from her to stand by the fireplace. "James called his father," he said, "who called the cops. Lucky for me, since by the time they showed up, Bart had damn near killed me."

"Where was your mother during all this?"

"Bart had locked her in the bedroom. Guess he wasn't taking any chances, but she wouldn't have done much anyway." Seeing her expression of disbelief, he said harshly, "She had to choose, and she chose him."

"I'm sorry." Hopelessly inadequate, it was all she knew to say. She crossed the room to him, put her hand on his arm, and squeezed, not letting him shake her off this time. "I'm so sorry," she repeated. She wanted to take him in her arms and soothe him, wanted to make his pain disappear, but she knew of no way to do it.

"Don't be. It turned out to be the best thing that could have happened to me. It got me out of that house. I lived with James's family until I graduated from high school and joined the navy. I never figured out why, but it didn't seem to bother the Bennetts that I was a terrorist's son."

"How did they find out? Did James tell them?"

"My stepfather did that, but I would have told them anyway. It wouldn't have been right to let them take me in not knowing. And it really chapped Bart's butt that they knew the truth and still let me live with them. But they were—" He paused and shook his head as if he still couldn't believe it. "They were something else. Good people."

"They loved you," Alex said softly.

"Yeah." He sounded surprised. "I guess they did."

She let her hand drop, wanting to offer more comfort but knowing he wasn't ready for it. To give him a chance to recover, to give herself something to focus on besides the horror of his adolescence, she said, "So five people actually knew the truth, not just three."

"Right. The Bennetts died in a car accident a few years back. But they wouldn't have come up with a plan like this. No, it fits James, and besides, he's the only one who could possibly be alive."

"I'm trying to understand how you and James went from being best friends, almost brothers, to him framing you in this bombing."

Wearily, he shoved a hand through his hair. He looked tired, she thought, and with the stubble of his beard shadowing his face and the remnants of anger in his gaze, he looked dangerous as well.

"Another long story, but I'll try to shorten it. James wasn't a bad kid, but he was greedy. Maybe my living with his family made it worse. Having to share his parents, as well as more material things."

"Did he resent you living with them?"

He tilted his head, considering. "Maybe subconsciously, he did resent me. But when I lived with them, I never knew it. And never felt it, not really."

"And after you grew up? Did he resent you then?"

As if it wasn't important, Luke shrugged. "Who can say? I'll tell you what he was like, though. James always wanted more. He wanted to make it big, he wanted it fast, and he didn't want to have to work too hard to get it."

"Did you know that when you became partners?"

"To some degree I'd always known it. But I wanted—or needed—to believe we could make a partnership work."

"And obviously, it didn't."

He shook his head. "At first it worked. Then he started substituting substandard material for the top grades we'd been contracted for. That led him eventually into attempting to bribe a public official. He expected me to back him up, because of our past. I didn't."

"Why not?"

Luke gave her an odd look, as if wondering why she'd asked him the question. "Because he was wrong. What he was doing was not only illegal, but unethical. Not to mention dangerous. My God, when I think what could have happened to those buildings if we hadn't found out—" He broke off and rubbed a hand over his face. "The point is, James was totally screwing up the firm. We were doing fine, there was no reason, other than greed, for him to do what he did. And his actions ended up wrecking my own career."

Again, Alex didn't know what to say. Luke had fallen silent and was simply standing, staring into the past, she imagined. She knew what that was like.

"I wish you'd felt that you could trust me with this," she said. "With your past."

He turned his head and gazed at her, and the naked emotion she saw glittering in his eyes tore at her heart. "I told you, it isn't a matter of trust. Not anymore."

"What is it, then?"

He touched her cheek, trailing his fingers down to her throat before letting his hand drop. "Telling you that my father was a terrorist is the last thing I ever wanted to do." He looked into her eyes and she caught a glimpse of bleak despair.

"Why?" she whispered.

"Because I'm in love with you, Alex."

ELEVEN

He hadn't expected the look of utter aston-
ishment that came over her face.

"You're . . . you . . ." Alex stared at him,
her eyes big and round with shock.

"I'm in love with you. Why do you look so
shocked? You must have had an idea."

"No." She shook her head, still looking
dazed. "No. I thought—I knew you . . .
wanted me, but I thought—I thought it was
just . . . sex."

His gaze locked with hers. "It was never
just sex for me. Not even the first time."

"For me either," she whispered.

Hope flared briefly in Luke, then died. It
didn't matter now. Now that she knew the
truth she would never . . . "So now you know
why I didn't tell you."

She frowned, looking puzzled. "No, I don't."

"Don't be naive," he said flatly. "You know exactly why."

Tilting her head, she fisted her hands on her hips. "Because of the investigation?"

"No, not because of the damned investigation, though that's a good reason too."

Incredulously, she asked, "Do you think I'd hold your birth against you? You have a strange idea of my character if that's what you believe."

"Not your character. Mine." He stretched his hand toward her, letting it fall before he touched her. If he touched her, he might not be able to let go. "Think about it, Alex. My father was a terrorist. A mass murderer. He didn't kill in the heat of passion, he planned his crimes in cold blood. Nineteen people died in the bombing he was convicted for. God knows how many others he had a part in, how many other people—men, women, children—he was responsible for killing. And I'm his son. His blood runs in my veins."

"It might run in your veins, but there's no blood on your hands."

"No?" He smiled bitterly. "What about the navy? Do you know what I did as a SEAL?"

"You were serving your country. That's different."

"I thought so too. At first."

"You can't possibly think you're like your father. You don't believe that, do you?"

He shrugged and turned away from her. "I sure as hell don't *want* to believe it. I've spent the last twenty years trying to prove I wasn't anything like him. That's why I joined the navy, and why I got out. It's why I became an architect, because I wanted to create instead of destroy. But I can't deny the facts."

"Facts?" she repeated. "What facts?" Grabbing hold of his arms, she tried to shake him. When she couldn't budge him, she thumped him on the chest with her fist. "You're what you've made of yourself. It has nothing at all to do with your father. Nothing."

He gazed into her eyes, so passionate, so earnest. "Can you stand there and tell me that you don't have a doubt about me? That knowing my past hasn't made you wonder if maybe I did blow up that building after all?"

"The only thing it makes me wonder"—her voice softened—"is how you became the man you are when you had so much going against you." She took a step closer, laying her palm against his cheek. Her eyes had grown tender, her mouth carried a loving smile. "No, it doesn't make me doubt you. I believe in you, Luke. I couldn't have fallen in love with you if I didn't."

He shut his eyes for a moment, holding her

words close. "Alex . . ." His voice trailed away. He didn't know what to say to her. Didn't know how to tell her what her words, or the sincerity behind them, meant to him. What her believing in him meant.

She pulled his head down to hers and kissed him. When he tried again to speak, she wrapped her arms around his neck and whispered, "Hush. Don't talk. Just kiss me, Luke." And then her lips were warm and giving against his.

Luke had never imagined telling a woman of his past. Never imagined a woman who, knowing the truth, wouldn't recoil in disgust. Instead of being sickened, Alex had kissed him. Instead of being repulsed, she was letting him know she wanted him.

She feathered another kiss across his lips, at the corners of his mouth, then back to seek and receive his tongue against hers. He could drown in her, he thought, wanted to drown in her.

Pulling back, he framed her face in his hands and stared into her eyes—deep blue eyes that had darkened to cobalt with the promise of passion. His hands were shaking, he saw, and wondered at it. He had never shaken for a woman before, never cared enough, or been reckless enough, to let a woman—to let any-one—get that close to him. But Alex had blasted his defenses to shreds from the time they'd met. First with her vulnerability, then with her strength. And now . . . with her love.

She didn't speak, but took his hand and led him to her bedroom. The top shutters were opened, moonlight spilling through the windows and illuminating the room, casting shadows across her bed. The sheets were rumpled and twisted, pillows spilled onto the floor, as though she'd been dreaming, or restlessly tossing, when his pounding on the door had roused her.

Standing beside the bed, she pulled his T-shirt from his jeans and pushed it upward. He jerked it the rest of the way off, flinging it aside. Her palms were warm against his chest as he tugged her belt open and slipped the robe off. She wore a nightgown beneath it, and he cupped her silk-covered breasts. She sighed and kissed his chest, her lips trailing across his skin to one nipple, then the other, circling and rasping her tongue over each one.

Her hand slid from his chest to his belly and below, caressing his erection through his jeans. He groaned and heard her soft laugh as she felt him grow even harder. She stepped away from him and swiftly drew her nightgown over her head, tossing it aside to stand before him, beautifully, gloriously naked.

Desire coiled tightly in his groin. Moonlight played over her pale skin, touching it as he was going to in a few short moments. But first he wanted to enjoy the sight of her, drink in all that creamy skin and gorgeous red hair flowing down to her shoulders and over her breasts. Her breasts were high and full, not extremely large, and to Luke's mind, they were perfect. Her dusky-rose nipples hardened as his gaze touched them, then lingered on her stomach, on the thatch of copper-red curls at the juncture of her thighs.

Her curves begged for a man's touch. His touch. He wanted to caress her, to taste her, to kiss her mouth, her breasts, her belly, to bury himself in her softness and hear her cry out his name at her climax.

"You are so beautiful," he said, knowing she'd heard it a thousand times before, but driven to say it anyway. He reached for her, bringing those luscious breasts to rest against his chest and groaning as the peaks burned an imprint into his skin and her scent surrounded him.

"So are you," she said.

"Men aren't beautiful," he muttered.

"You are." She kissed his mouth, darting her tongue everywhere, teasing him, taunting him.

His hands slid to her hips, to cup and caress, to hold her tightly against his own raging ache. He lowered his head to kiss her breasts, to draw her nipples into his mouth and suckle each one in turn.

She pushed away from him, her hands on the fly of his jeans. He was so hard, he knew she'd have trouble getting him unzipped, but he couldn't bring himself to stop her, or to help, either. Her struggles, her gasps of laughter and his, only increased the pleasure. Finally, she had his jeans undone and she helped him push them down his hips, barely waiting for him to step out of them before she shoved him back on the bed and followed him, her body warm and pliant against his.

Her hand closed around him, stroking his bare flesh until he was more aroused than he'd ever been in his life and his single, driving thought was to get inside her. He started to roll over, to pin her beneath him, but she stopped him with a laugh muffled against his skin.

"No way. This time I'm seducing you."

He pulled her head up and kissed her mouth. "I can live with that." But as her hands and mouth played over him, he wasn't sure that he could.

When he was hanging on to his control by a whisper, she straddled him, sliding down on him inch by slow inch, until he was sunk to the hilt inside her. She was tight. Hot. Wet, She was killing him, but God, what a way to die. He stroked her breasts as she rode him, watched her face as her arousal shimmered in her half-closed eyes and rippled across her skin.

She threw her head back and pressed her hips against his, taking him deeper. Her muscles tightened, clamping down on him in a velvet vise, and he felt her climax vibrate through her. Grasping her hips, he drove himself upward and came in long, hard waves, pouring himself into her, hearing her call his name as she peaked.

He could barely breathe, much less move, but he managed to tug her head back from where she lay collapsed on his chest and kiss her ripe, willing mouth. "I love you, Alex."

She smiled, looking unbelievably sweet and sexy as sin. "I love you, Luke."

He kissed her again and wondered, if just this once, he might keep the happiness. Keep Alex. Or would it blow up in his face like every other dream he'd ever had?

Considering the lack of sleep, Alex felt surprisingly good the next morning. Must be love, she thought, smiling. And a hot shower didn't hurt either.

"I used your razor and some toothpaste," Luke said, coming into the kitchen. "You'll be happy to know I left your toothbrush alone." He bent to brush a kiss across her lips.

She smiled. "Oh, I am. What did you use instead?"

He held up his index finger. "I improvised."

Laughing, she waved at the box of granola on the kitchen table. "Help yourself."

Grimacing, he poured a cup of coffee and took a seat. "Too healthy for me. Don't you have something loaded with fat and sugar? Doughnuts come to mind."

"My body is a temple," she said, and took a dainty bite of cereal.

He gave her a rakish look. "That it is. And a gorgeous temple, at that."

She laughed and shook her head. "It's too early for a line like that."

"Sweetheart"—he smiled devilishly —"it's never too early for a good line."

He was good with lines, and with women, she thought, remembering the first time she met him. Smooth, but not pushy. Of course, she hadn't exactly fought off his advances. Frowning, she wondered for a moment about the women in his past. She knew there'd been women. Possibly a lot of women. He hadn't mentioned them, though, not one.

"What are you thinking?" he asked, pouring milk over his cereal.

"I'm wondering about the women in your past," she said, deciding to tell him the truth. "And why you haven't mentioned any."

"There haven't been any." He took a bite of cereal and shot her a quick glance.

Alex snorted in disbelief.

Luke grinned, then sobered. "No one important. Until you."

She found that she believed him, and hoped it wasn't because she was so hopelessly bedazzled that she'd believe anything he told her.

"What about you?" he asked. "How many men have you left with a broken heart?"

"Scores of them," she said lightly, smiling when he picked up her hand and kissed it. "But there hasn't been anyone important. Until you."

His eyes darkened and she saw desire flash in them, but he only smiled and squeezed her hand.

Alex waited until he'd started on his second cup of coffee before she brought up the subject she'd been pondering all morning. "I put in a call to talk to the St. Petersburg, Florida, Police Department. Specifically, to the officer in charge of the scene of the plane crash. I want to see a copy of the police reports."

Luke's expression hardened. "I don't think they'll do you much good."

"Maybe not, but it's a start. There's got to be some way of proving James Bennett is alive. I'm going to need several things from you. A description of Bennett, first off. Or a photo would be even better. Although he's almost certainly changed his appearance, it will help us to get an idea of his build and coloring."

"I can probably scare up a photo. What else do you need from me?"

"A list of his friends, family, favorite haunts. Bars, restaurants, health clubs, any-place he used to frequent."

"I can give it to you, but—do you think he's in town hanging out at his favorite bar? What about the risk of someone recognizing him?"

"As I said, I imagine he's changed his looks. I think he's close, Luke. The nature of the crime indicates he wants to see you suffer rather than see you dead. He wants you in jail, suffering like he was supposed to be. Isn't it likely that he'd want to be near to see your downfall?"

Cradling his coffee mug in his hands, he appeared to be thinking that over. "Yeah," he said after a long moment. "James would want to be in on the kill. He's close, all right."

"So if we're going to track him down, I need to know everything you can tell me about him. Is he married?"

"Divorced. He blames me for that too." He sipped his coffee and set the mug down.

"Why?" She hoped . . . No, Luke didn't seem the type to have an affair with his best friend's wife.

"She divorced him when the crap hit the

fan. He refused to believe that she'd been on the verge of divorcing him for two years before that. In his mind, if I hadn't betrayed him, if he hadn't been indicted, she'd never have left him."

"Would he try to contact her?"

"I doubt it. She made it clear she didn't want anything to do with him after the divorce. They didn't have any kids, so there was nothing still binding them. Besides, she moved to California a few months ago."

"If you can think of anyone he might turn to, let me know."

He shook his head. "James was a loner. He didn't let a lot of people close. But I'll think on it."

Alex checked the time and groaned. She needed to get to the station. "I'm beyond late, but there are a couple of other things I need to ask you. Does Bennett know explosives?"

"No. He knows structural engineering, though, so he'd have known where to set the bomb. Maybe he picked up some knowledge of demolitions. Or maybe he hired someone to do it. If I know James, he had money stashed somewhere."

"What about that electronic transfer? Could he have done that?"

"Maybe." Luke shrugged. "That's something right up his alley, anyway. He was a hacker. Pretty damn good at it too."

"Call me later with those details, okay?" She rose as Luke did, but he stopped her with a hand on her arm.

"Alex, last night you said you'd put your career on the line for me. I don't want this— my problems—to endanger your career. I've been on the receiving end of a wrecked career and I don't intend for that to happen to you."

She touched his cheek. "It's my choice. My investigation. The captain trusts me to get the job done, and that's what I intend to do."

Luke pulled her into his arms and kissed her, a long, thorough kiss that revved up her heartbeat and had her wishing they could simply crawl back into bed and ignore all the problems that awaited them.

"We're going to find him," she said, "and nail him."

TWELVE

A couple of days later, Alex ran into her brother on the steps of the police station as she was starting her shift and he was obviously ending his. Noticing his rumpled clothing and the stubble of his beard, she decided he must have pulled an all-nighter.

"Hey, Nick. Bad night?"

Passing a hand over bloodshot eyes, he groaned tiredly. "Don't ask. You don't want to know."

He was probably right about that, Alex thought, which was one of the reasons she'd decided on the bomb unit rather than homicide. Not that the bomb unit was stress-free, but Alex didn't think she could deal with some of the things her brother had to handle on at least a semidaily basis.

"So," he said, taking her arm and walking

her back down the steps, toward his car, which was parked by the curb. "How's your investigation going?"

"Better, I guess." Discussing the plane crash with the St. Petersburg police lieutenant who had been in charge of the accident site had not only confirmed that James Bennett's body had never been found, it had left her more certain than ever that he was behind the bombing of the Alsobrook building. Still, she had yet to find any indication of where Bennett might be.

She sighed and said, "The problem is, I'm looking for a dead man."

"Come again?"

"A dead man. I know, it sounds crazy. But my major suspect right now is a man believed to be dead."

"But you think he's alive." Nick leaned back against the car and crossed his arms over his chest.

"Yes." She said it somewhat defiantly, but Nick only scrubbed a hand over the back of his neck and groaned.

"Got any facts to back it up?"

"Not exactly. But I will soon." Nick snorted and she continued. "Listen to this scenario, though. This guy—his name's James Bennett—supposedly died in a plane crash off the Florida Gulf Coast. Fact number one, though, is that his body was never found. I talked to the St. Petersburg Police Department, to the lieutenant in charge of the crash scene. From his description, I'm sure nothing would have been easier than for this guy to leave the scene and assume a new identity."

"Why would he do that?"

"He was about to go to jail for bribing a public official and fraud."

Nick nodded thoughtfully. "Okay, so far, so good. But can you establish motive for him blowing up your building?"

Alex considered him for a minute. Technically, she shouldn't be discussing the case with him, but he wouldn't discuss it with anyone else and she needed a sounding board she could trust.

"I think he's trying to frame someone else for the crime," she said.

"Uh-huh." Nick gave her a sardonic glance. "Let me guess. This 'someone else' wouldn't be the mysterious suspect you're not exactly involved with, now, would it?"

She couldn't help smiling. "No, Luke Morgan happens to be the suspect I'm in love with."

Caught in mid-yawn, Nick choked. "In *love* with?" he repeated, his tone making it sound like a fatal disease. "Good God, Alex, get a grip. You're not even supposed to be involved with this guy, much less"—he shuddered—"in love with him. Your butt is gonna be in a sling for this one."

"I know. But I don't care." That wasn't precisely true, but there wasn't anything she could do about her feelings. She was in love with Luke and she intended to prove his innocence. "I've got a lot of circumstantial evidence that points to Luke being involved. And I've got to find something concrete to prove he's not."

Nick's expression was somber as he looked at her. "What if he's guilty? Have you thought about what you're going to do if you're wrong?"

"No." She shook her head firmly. "He's not the bomber, Nick. I know it and I'm going to prove it. But I've got to find James Bennett in order to do it."

"Good luck. Sounds like you're going to need it." As Alex left him to go inside he called after her, "Maybe it's just the night I had, but I've got a bad feeling you're going to get burned on this one, Alex."

"You worry too much, Nick," she answered, but she was worried too. For the first time in her life, she was in love, but the man she'd fallen in love with was in serious trouble. Trouble that she had to help him out of. It was a scary feeling to a woman who'd always been independent to know that so much of her happiness hinged on another person. That what happened to the other person could matter so much.

The past few nights since Luke had opened up to her had been wonderful. Not just the lovemaking, but simply being with him, talking to him. She felt connected to him in a way she'd never felt to anyone before. But there was a cloud hanging over their future, and that cloud was the Alsobrook bombing. Until she solved this case, until she discovered if James Bennett really was alive and framing Luke, their future would be on hold.

"Hey, Alex." Crukshank, one of her team members, called to her as she walked into the squad room. "Got a tip a little earlier I think you'll want to hear."

"Mmm. What was it?" she asked, sifting through the mess on her desk. Another tip. She wondered if this one would be any more productive than the others had been. So far it had been one dead end after another, but that was often the nature of tips.

"They want us to check out the architect's office. Our tipster says we'll find explosives on the premises."

Her hands froze on her mail. Heart pounding, she raised her head and speared him with a glance. "Who called it in?"

"Anonymous." Crukshank rolled his eyes. "Are they ever anything else? But I thought you'd want to know since the architect is one of the suspects you've been following."

"Yes, thanks." She sank into her chair, her

mind alive with the implications, her emotions in a tumult. On the one hand, this could be the break she'd been waiting for. James Bennett was the tipster, she'd bet a month's pay on it. But why had he called the tip in now? He had to be wondering why Luke hadn't been arrested, given the circumstantial evidence against him. Maybe he was getting tired of waiting and wanted to force the issue.

And he *had* forced the issue, Alex admitted. She no longer had a choice about her next move. Given what she knew about the case so far, she couldn't in good conscience ignore the tip. She would have to search Luke's office. Assuming they found evidence of explosives there—and she didn't doubt they would—she would have to arrest him and charge him with the crime. After all, Bennett would hardly have called if he hadn't planted something worthwhile for the police to find.

She would have to do some fancy talking and rely heavily on her reputation in order to convince the district attorney that they didn't have enough evidence against Luke to convict him. Depending on what she found in Luke's office, that might be difficult. If at all possible, she didn't want to formally charge him. Arresting him and bringing him in for questioning would be bad enough.

The first thing she needed to do was lay everything before her captain and hope that he agreed with her assessment that Luke was being framed. If she knew the captain, he'd chew her out from here to Tuesday for not coming to him sooner with her suspicions, but since all the evidence had been circumstantial up to this point, hopefully he'd leave her a few strips of hide when he finished with her. After that, she'd work on securing a search warrant for Luke's office.

But what was Luke going to do when she arrested him? She had to hope that he would understand what she was doing and why. That he would see that she had no choice in what she did. That he wouldn't see her searching his office and bringing him in as a betrayal.

Betrayal. She had a grim, cold feeling that was exactly how he'd see it. And there was nothing, absolutely nothing she could do to soften the blow.

Late that afternoon Luke heard a commotion in his outer office. Irritated, he stalked to the door, intending to ask his secretary what the hell she meant by allowing a riot while he was trying to work. Jerking open the door, he halted in mid-question at the sight of Alex and two uniformed officers.

His eyebrows lifted in surprise. "Alex? Is there a problem?"

Her face expressionless, her voice dead

calm, she said, "I have a warrant to search the premises."

"Search the premises?" he repeated, confused. "What for?" Their gazes met. He could read nothing in her eyes. They were as cold and lifeless as three-day-dead ashes.

"Evidence of explosive materials." She handed him a paper, turned away, and spoke to one of the officers. "Croft, you and I will start with Mr. Morgan's office. Douglas, you can get to work out here."

Luke stared down at the piece of paper in his hands. A search warrant, all nice and tidy. He understood what it was, but he couldn't take in, couldn't comprehend Alex's actions. "What the hell is going on?" he demanded as they pushed past him into his office.

"Standard search, sir," the one she'd called Croft said. "This may take a while. You'd best go sit down."

Luke made a crude comment, telling him what he could do with his suggestion. The officer started toward him, but Alex halted him with a sharp word.

"Don't touch anything and don't get in the way," she said to Luke.

Cold, calm, detached. The consummate police detective at work, he thought. Completely unlike the woman who had come alive in his arms night after night. No trace of that woman existed in the one standing before him.

He wanted to drag her out of there and demand she talk to him, but he had a sick feeling that he wouldn't like her explanation.

She resumed her search.

Luke leaned a shoulder against the doorjamb, stuffed his hands in his pockets so he wouldn't be tempted to hit somebody, and watched Alex destroy him.

He watched her, unable to believe that she could erase the woman behind the professional so completely. Not by so much as a stammer did she betray that she was on anything other than a routine search and seizure. She did her job, efficiently, bloodlessly, almost silently, neither looking at him nor speaking to him.

Had it all been a fake? Had her every move since meeting him again been designed to seduce a confession out of him? He could hardly believe it, yet the evidence was forming before his eyes.

Sometime later, after Alex and the officer had finished with his desk and had started on the wooden lateral files lining one wall, he heard Croft say, "Bingo."

Alex pulled a package from the bottom of the file cabinet, underneath the drawer and another piece of wood that must have been a false bottom. Luke didn't have to inspect it to know it contained explosives or, at the least, explosive accessories—blasting caps, fuses, detonating cord. Whatever it was, it would be incriminating as hell.

She bagged the bulky package in a paper bag. He heard her telling the officer to dust the cabinet and everything in it for fingerprints, while two thoughts inundated his mind, as insistent and pervasive as Chinese water torture.

James had won.

Alex had betrayed him.

He kept his gaze on her face the entire time she read him his rights, willed her to look him in the eye as she cuffed him. She didn't.

Driven to get some kind of response from her, he asked, "I guess the end justifies the means, doesn't it, Alex?" He heard the cuffs click closed.

For a moment, just an instant, she lifted her gaze to his and he thought he saw regret in her eyes. Then they became shuttered again. No, he knew better. The only thing Alex regretted was the lengths she'd had to go to to get the evidence.

And through it all, a black, numbing fury beat in his blood and ate at his soul. Rage, that he could have trusted her. Disgust, that he had been so gullible as to think she believed him— and that he had spilled his guts to her. Disbelief, that he could have fallen in love with a woman who could make passionate love with him one moment and arrest him the next.

Without a glimmer of emotion. Without a hint of conscience.

As if they'd never been lovers. As if she'd never sworn she loved him, never sworn she believed in him.

As if her actions hadn't destroyed him more completely than any scheme of James's ever could.

Alex had known nothing would be harder than searching Luke's office and arresting him. The only way she'd managed to do it at all had been to treat him and the situation totally impersonally. She'd been prepared to see him turn on her in anger. She had understood his feelings, had believed she could deal with them because she knew she'd had no other choice but to act as she had. And she also knew that she would do everything in her power to see that Luke walked out without ever being formally charged with the crime.

She wanted so badly to explain what was going on, to beg him to trust her, to understand that her plan would draw James Bennett out as nothing else would. As a detective, though, she could tell him nothing. And it was the detective who would have to question him.

She drew in a deep breath, straightened her shoulders, and walked into the interrogation room. Luke's wrists were cuffed, his hands clasped together on the table in front of him. His lawyer sat beside him, frowning at a piece of paper in his hands.

"Illegal search and seizure," the lawyer was muttering as she came in.

"I don't think so," Alex said. "Take those cuffs off," she told the officer standing beside the two men. To Luke, she said, "I'd like to ask you some questions."

"I've advised my client—"

"Ask what you want," Luke interrupted. "But if you're expecting a confession, you can forget it."

The look of disgust he gave her shamed her, but it made her angry as well. After all they'd shared, couldn't he trust her a little? Didn't he understand she had to do her job? Didn't he know she would do everything in her power to see that he wasn't framed?

Obviously not, she thought as his contemptuous gaze raked her up and down. She raised her chin and spoke as coldly, as dispassionately, as she could manage. "You have denied all knowledge of the package of explosive accessories found underneath your file cabinet. Is that correct?"

"Yes."

Alex wondered how he managed to communicate such anger with a single word, but she felt it like a blast of heat. She had faced this kind of anger before, in some of the perpetrators she'd sent to prison. But she'd never had to deal with it from someone she cared about. Never had to take it from the man she loved.

"Do you have any explanation for how the material came to be there?"

"No."

So, he didn't intend to mention that he thought he was being framed. "No explanation at all? Not even a guess?"

"No."

"Has your office been broken into recently?"

"No."

She gritted her teeth, aware he was doing his best to infuriate her, and that he was succeeding. "Can you give me a list of people who might have had access to your office?"

He shrugged. "Why should I bother?"

"Just do it," she snapped. To his lawyer she said, "It would be in your client's best interests to cooperate with the police. I suggest you tell him that."

"Thanks but no thanks, Detective," Luke said harshly. "I've seen how much good cooperating has done me." He rose, pinning her with a glare. "I'm all talked out. You have any more to say, tell it to my lawyer."

Alex worked late that evening, hoping that hard work would hold the memories of the past several hours at bay. It didn't. Her mind wouldn't stay focused on the job. Instead she kept seeing Luke's face when he realized she'd come to arrest him, or the way he'd looked at her when she was questioning him. She knew she was in for a long, miserable night.

Around ten her phone rang. "Sheridan."

"This is fingerprints, Detective. I've got some results for you."

"Go ahead," she said, and held her breath. She knew they wouldn't find Luke's prints on the package. In fact, she doubted they would find any prints at all, but she still held to a faint hope that she might get a break in the case.

"There were no prints on the exterior of the package, but we did find one print on a blasting cap."

"Whose is it?"

"Well, it's not the suspect's. We don't know yet whose it is."

Joy swept through her. Barely containing her excitement, she said, "I've got a good idea who it belongs to. His name is James Bennett. He's been convicted, so his prints should be easily accessed."

"Will do. I take it you want the results of this as soon as possible also?"

It was late and he sounded tired, but Alex really didn't care. "Yes. Thanks a lot."

With any luck, she might even manage to

get Luke released that night. Then she could talk to him—away from the station and the constraints of her job.

But would he listen to anything she had to say?

THIRTEEN

Spending the night in jail hadn't improved Luke's mood. Being taken to see Alex early the next morning didn't help it either. He noticed the dark circles beneath her eyes and hoped she'd spent as miserable a night as he had, but he doubted it. Her conscience sure hadn't kept her up—yesterday had proved she didn't have one.

"Isn't my lawyer supposed to be present?" he asked, taking the chair she indicated.

She met his gaze levelly. "If you were being charged, yes. But since I'm releasing you, I didn't think you'd care."

It was the last thing he'd expected to hear her say. "You're releasing me."

"That's what I said. You're free to go."

"Just like that." Eyes narrowed, he stared at her. "What's your game now?"

Her control slipped a little and her voice rose. "I'm not playing games, I'm doing my job. Which is what I've been doing all along." She stretched a hand out toward him, then checked herself. "I'd like to take you home. Talk to you. I can explain—"

He laughed, but he wasn't amused. "Forget it, Alex. I'm nowhere near that gullible. Not anymore."

"If you'll just hear me out . . ."

He looked into her gorgeous blue eyes, glinting with the sheen of what he could swear were tears. She was good, he admitted. Really good. "Save it. The last thing I need to hear is more lies from you."

"I haven't lied to you. I meant everything I said."

"Do you really expect me to believe you? After what you did?"

Her gaze met his, then faltered. "I know you're angry and—and hurt, but please. Give me a chance to explain."

Hurt? Angry? She'd destroyed him and now she expected him to give her another shot at him? "You want to talk to me, arrest me. Again."

Her jaw clenched. She didn't speak for a minute, and when she did, her voice was low so that he had to strain to hear it above the noise in the station room. "I'd have given anything not to have had to arrest you. But I had no choice."

"Tell it to some other fool," he said, disgusted with her for saying it, and more, with himself for wanting to listen to her.

Thirty minutes later, he sat in Waylon Black's truck, anticipating the oblivion of a hot shower. "Thanks for picking me up."

"Not a problem. What happened? I talked to your secretary yesterday, but she didn't know much beyond the bare bones. Why did Detective Sheridan arrest you? I thought she'd decided you weren't a suspect."

"She changed her mind," Luke said bitterly.

Waylon shook his head. "You know, for a while there I had the feeling she was liking me for it." He shot Luke a sharp glance.

Since Luke had no desire to tell Waylon he'd suspected him, too, he said nothing.

"So what changed her mind?" Waylon continued. "I thought you two had something going."

Yeah, they'd had something going. But it wasn't what Luke had thought it was. Every time he remembered how Alex had taken him in, how damn good she'd been, he wanted to put his fist through a wall. And he'd had plenty of time to brood over his stupidity while he lay on the hard bunk of a jail cell all night. "Long story, which I'm not up for."

As he'd expected, Waylon didn't take the hint. "She sure looked upset when you left. I looked back at her and she was staring after you like a lost puppy. Seems funny to me that if the two of you were an item that she'd be ready to—"

"Waylon," Luke interrupted. "Shut up."

"Well, okay, if that's the way you want it, but it seems to me . . ."

He kept talking. Luke managed to block out the words, wishing it was as easy to stop Alex's image from filling his mind. Or to stop the seductive sound of her voice, begging him to let her explain. As if he could believe anything she said now.

She was a liar—a cop prepared to do anything necessary as long as it gave her someone to pin the crime on. And the worst part of it, the part he couldn't stomach, was that he was still in love with her.

Alex gave Luke the rest of the day and the night before she tried to contact him again. She knew it would be difficult getting him to listen to her, but she hoped that a good night's sleep and time to think things over might make him a little more willing to hear her out.

Early in the morning before he left for work, she called him at home.

"Luke?" Lucky he'd answered the phone, she thought. She'd been afraid he wouldn't.

"What do you want?" His voice was harsh, cold, and more like steel than ever.

"To talk to you." Her hand tightened on the receiver as she waited for his answer, praying he was ready to listen.

"Is this police business?"

"No, but I—" She heard a click, then a dial tone and realized she was talking to air.

So much for a good night's sleep changing his attitude, she thought. Hanging up on her expressed his feelings pretty clearly. She redialed, this time getting his machine. Though she didn't hold any hope that he'd return her call, she left a message anyway.

Later that morning she tried him again, this time at his office.

"Two Thousand A.D. Architectural," a nasal voice answered.

Great, Alex thought. His secretary who had hated her *before* the search. At her most professional, she said, "Luke Morgan, please."

"May I tell him who's calling?"

No, she wanted to say. "Alex Sheridan."

"One moment." She came back on the line in less than thirty seconds. "He wants to know if this is official business."

Tempted to lie, Alex gritted her teeth. "No. However, it's very important that—"

The secretary interrupted her in a clipped,

businesslike tone that managed to hold amused satisfaction. "Mr. Morgan says that if you want to talk to him, you can arrest him. Otherwise he has nothing to say to you."

A click and she was talking to the atmosphere again. Alex slammed the receiver down and rose to pace around her desk. He wasn't going to get away with this. She smacked her fist against her palm. His feelings were understandable, but she was damned if she'd do nothing while he refused even to speak to her.

By God, she decided, he was going to listen to her if she had to handcuff them together to get him to do it.

Feeling like he'd aged ten years in the last couple of days, Luke dragged himself up the stairs to his second-story apartment. As he reached the top he saw Alex waiting by his door. His gaze flickered over her as she straightened and moved away from the wall.

"Where's the warrant?"

She gave him a long, unsmiling look. "I don't have one. I didn't come to arrest you, I came to talk to you."

"That's your problem. I don't want to talk to you."

"You've made that obvious." She fisted her hands on her hips, thrust her chin out, and glared at him. "And that's too damn bad. You're *going* to listen to me."

Like hell he was, he thought. "Threats? Harassment?" he asked with a smile calculated to infuriate her. "Why, Detective, I'm shocked."

"Tell it to your lawyer."

Turning his back on her, he stuck the key in the lock.

She slapped a palm on the door. "I'm coming in."

He shrugged and opened the door, leaving her to follow. Once inside, he tossed his briefcase on the small table by the front door, then tugged off his tie and threw it on top of the briefcase. Still without a word to her, he walked into the kitchen. Short of throwing her out bodily, he didn't know how to get rid of her, but he damned sure didn't have to talk to her.

Moments later, he came out carrying a beer bottle and sprawled on the couch. Downing a good third of his beer, he reached for the remote control to the TV and flipped it on.

Alex stalked over, ripped the remote out of his hand, aimed it at the screen, and jammed her thumb on the off button. After tossing the remote over her shoulder, she placed a hand on either side of him and leaned close until she was right in his face.

Her eyes glinting angrily, she said, "I'm not

leaving until you've listened to what I have to say."

He'd never hit a woman in his life and he didn't intend to start now. But that didn't mean he had his temper or anything else under control. "Back off, Alex," he warned her. "You don't want to push me right now."

They measured each other silently. She backed away from him, but otherwise stood her ground.

He could tell by the stubborn look on her face that she wouldn't leave until she'd had her say. "Say what you want and get out."

She didn't speak immediately, but took a seat in the easy chair beside the couch. "We received an anonymous tip telling us to search your office. Combined with the circumstantial evidence against you, I was forced to give the DA everything that I had on the case. He ordered the search warrant. Once we found the package, there was nothing else I could do but bring you in."

"Poor Alex," he mocked. "Torn between duty and"—he stopped and looked her over insultingly—"obviously not love, so it must be sex."

She paled, appearing more fragile than he'd seen her look since she'd arrested him. "I do love you, even if you're not willing to believe that."

"Sorry, Detective. The evidence indicates otherwise."

Her jaw tightened and she leaned forward in the chair. "If you could be objective for a minute, you might see that this is a break for us."

He laughed harshly. "It's a break all right. For you. Makes it easy to pin the crime on me, doesn't it?"

"If I was so eager to slap this on you, would I have released you? How do you explain that?"

"Lack of evidence." He shrugged. "The package is circumstantial evidence unless you've got some way to tie me to it. Evidently you don't or I'd be in jail on a terrorism charge."

"You're acting like I wanted to arrest you. Like I wanted you to be guilty."

He remembered how calm she'd been, how emotionless. "It didn't seem to bother you at the time."

"Of course it bothered me! I'm in love with you. But I had to—I had to do my job. No matter what it did to me, or what it did to you. I couldn't let my feelings for you interfere. That doesn't mean it was easy for me to do it. And it doesn't mean that I believed for a minute that you had anything to do with that package or anything to do with bombing the Alsobrook building."

God, he must be a fool. He wanted to believe her, so badly. But he'd believed her before, and she'd betrayed him.

Or had she?

He remembered when he'd told her about his father. How she'd kissed him. Told him she loved him. Made love with him. Could she have faked those emotions? Or had she just bewitched him to the point that he couldn't tell lies from reality?

She continued. "James Bennett's fingerprint was found on one of the blasting caps in the package. He planted that package and then he called the tip in. But he was cocky and careless and left a print. I was able to convince the DA that we don't have enough evidence against you. He's not quite convinced yet that you're being framed, but I'm working on him."

It sounded logical. Reasonable. But it would, of course, because Alex was too smart to come up with a story that didn't sound reasonable.

"So I'm supposed to be grateful to you now."

"You're *supposed* to understand that what's happened is going to flush James Bennett out of hiding. What do you think he'll do when he discovers you were never even charged with the crime?"

"Why don't you tell me, since you've figured out all the angles?"

Banked excitement sparkled in her eyes. "He'll make another move. He's bound to. And when he does, the police are going to be there waiting for him."

"Meaning what?"

"I've got men staked out here, at the bomb site, and at your office. All we have to do is wait for Bennett to get anxious, which judging by his behavior these past few days should be soon, and then we nail him. Don't you see, Luke? This is our chance to get Bennett. To clear you for good."

He stared at her, not knowing what to think. She looked so damn sincere, and more, she looked afraid. Afraid that he wouldn't buy the story?

What was her plan? Was she trying to get him to trust her again, knowing she'd lost all credibility when she arrested him? Did she think he was that stupid?

Maybe he *was* that stupid.

She came to sit beside him, put her hand on his arm. He wished she wouldn't touch him, because he found it hard to think clearly when she did. He wished he didn't want to believe her, wished that she didn't matter a damn to him, instead of meaning so much he was willing to do almost anything if it meant having her again.

Almost anything. Even risk betrayal . . . again?

"Think about it, Luke. Why would I be here now, if I thought you were guilty? Why would I have told you about my people watching you, if I didn't believe in your innocence?"

"I don't know." He clenched his fist, fighting the need to slam it into the wall. "Dammit, I don't know."

"You don't want to believe me, do you? Why are you so afraid to trust me?"

Because when she had betrayed him, it had hurt worse than anything he could remember, including finding out about his father. And if he were to trust her, believe her again, and then find out he'd been wrong . . .

It would destroy him for good.

She put her arms around him. Kissed him. Whispered she loved him. He didn't respond, couldn't allow himself to, because he knew if he did, he'd be lost. He grabbed her arms and held her away from him.

"Sex won't work, Alex. Not this time."

Pain flooded her face, and he felt a brief surge of shame before the anger took over.

"Get out." He forced the words out through a tight throat. "Get the hell out."

"I wasn't trying to seduce you."

"Right. Get out, Alex. You've had your say."

She didn't say anything else, but when she

got to the door, she turned around and looked at him. He could have sworn he saw her heart in her eyes.

He didn't call her back. But he wanted to. God, he wanted to.

FOURTEEN

Alex dropped her head onto the steering wheel and cursed herself for being a fool. Why had she kissed him? Things were going badly enough before that, but kissing Luke had been such a *stupid* thing to do. Of course he'd have seen it as an attempt at seduction rather than for what it was, an expression of love. Which he didn't for a minute believe.

Straightening, she stared blindly out the windshield before letting her head fall back against the seat. She should go to her apartment, she knew, instead of sitting out in the complex's parking lot as an advertisement for a mugging. But her limbs were leaden, her heart suffocated. Every moment felt like she was swimming in wet cement.

Maybe he'd change his mind. Maybe he'd think over what she'd said and forgive her for what he saw as her betrayal. She remembered how cold and empty his face had looked when she left. Hard as a rock, unforgiving as a steel girder.

Forgive her? She'd have to be delusional to believe that would ever happen. And Alex had always been a realist.

She forced herself to get out of the car. An uneasy tingle prickled up her spine. Her hand tightened around her keys. Normally, the lot was well lit, but tonight two lights were out. The ones nearest her parking space. Coincidence, she told herself, but apprehension still danced along her skin.

Footsteps rang out from behind her. She started to turn and a stinging blow slammed into her shoulder, an outrageous slash of pain. She sagged to her knees, gasping for breath. Her arm numb, she fumbled for the pepper spray on the end of her key chain. Tried to aim it, saw his fist coming at her face. She threw her arm up and blocked it. He grabbed her with his other hand and pulled her in front of him, her back to his front. His arm encircled her neck and he started to choke her.

She jammed her elbow into his abdomen, her full strength behind it. Drove the high heel of her shoe into the vulnerable top of his foot. He shouted a curse and his hold loosened, though just barely. Ripping free, she started to run and let out a scream that could have been heard across the Trinity River.

Her head snapped back as he grabbed her hair, yanked her back against him. Tears of pain mingled with rage and stung at her eyes. She smelled fear. Hers. And pain. She hoped viciously that it was his as well. One of his arms wrapped around her waist and lifted her, his other hand covering her mouth as he tried to muzzle her.

Alex bit down savagely and kicked him. He jerked his hand away and spoke for the first time. "Dammit, you bit me, you bitch!"

He dropped her with a jarring thud. Grabbing her again, he turned her around, his fingers stabbing into her skin, his hold tightening until she had to bite back a cry of agony. Unable to move her arms, she lashed out with her foot again and caught him in the thigh. It barely checked him. His fist smashed into her chin.

She saw stars, a black swirling mist, and then . . . nothing.

Alex came to sometime later to find herself in a car with her attacker driving. She was handcuffed to the door, her jaw hurt like a root canal, and pure fear tore at her with icy fangs. She could see the headlines now: BOMB-UNIT IN-VESTIGATOR FOUND RAPED AND MURDERED.

Her entire body screamed with aches. Before she could stop herself, she moaned.

"Awake, are you?" her attacker asked.

She turned her head to look at him, but her mind was still foggy and she couldn't see him very well. Keep him talking, she thought, remembering rape-prevention classes. But the best prevention, she was grimly aware, would have been to have her gun in a shoulder holster, instead of in her purse. "I'm a cop. When I don't check in, there's going to be an immediate search. I'm working on a—"

He laughed, cutting her off. "I know exactly what you're working on, Detective Sheridan. But you should have paid more attention to your job instead of sleeping with the prime suspect."

Her head felt fuzzy. Willing her vision to clear, she stared at him. Blond hair, fairly good-looking. Familiar, but she could have sworn she'd never met him. Yet he knew her name. He knew . . . Oh, God. It couldn't be. . . .

"If you'd just put Luke in jail where he belongs," James Bennett said, "this wouldn't have happened. But now you're going to have to help me."

Desperately, she tried to force herself to think clearly. "If you let me go, I can see if—"

"Let you go?" he interrupted, laughing again. "You're my bait, lady. I think Luke's going to be real interested to know that his cop lover's got a date with a car bomb. Don't you think so?"

Her stomach rolled and plummeted to her toes. How did he know? How could he know about Luke and her? "He's not my lover."

Bennett snorted. "I saw you coming out of his apartment at six in the morning, wearing the same clothes you had on the night before. You expect me to believe you two were playing Monopoly all night?" He shot her a lewd glance and smiled. "Gotta admit, Luke always did have good taste in women."

"It was nothing. A one-night—"

He stopped her denial with a foul word. "You two have been hot and heavy for days now. I've been watching him—and that means I've been watching you too. He's got it bad for you, lady, and I'm going to use that. He'll do anything I want him to when I tell him about you. You just watch."

"No. He won't."

"What do you mean, no? Once he hears I've got you, he'll go where I tell him quicker than you can spit."

"No, he won't," she said again, but she knew she sounded too desperate. She willed her voice to level out. "Luke hates me now. He thinks I betrayed him when I arrested him."

"Give me a break. You let the SOB out. He was never even charged. I know, I checked."

"He doesn't care. I'm telling you, he won't come for me." But he would. She knew he would. Even if he never forgave her, he wouldn't leave her to Bennett. It simply wasn't in Luke's nature to evade responsibility—and he would feel responsible for Bennett's abducting her. But maybe she could convince Bennett that he hated her enough that he wouldn't care.

"You'd better pray he does come," Bennett said.

"Let me go and I can make things easier on you. Kidnapping is a felony."

He shrugged. "So's bribing a public official. So's bombing a building. What's one more charge?" He glanced at her and smiled widely. "Especially to a dead man."

Her stomach churned with nausea. He'd just admitted to bombing the Alsobrook building. In the presence of a police officer.

He was going to kill her.

And make Luke watch? Or kill them both?

He'd done what he'd set out to do, Luke thought, and driven Alex away. He should have been happy, or failing that, at peace. Peace. What a joke. Until he got Alex out of his system, he'd never have peace.

And he didn't believe he'd ever get her out of his system.

He hadn't moved since she left, hadn't done anything but sit and think and remember. Remember everything they'd talked about. Remember what she'd looked like every time they made love. He didn't believe, in either his heart or his mind, that Alex could be that good an actress.

She loved him and he'd told her to get the hell out of his life.

He heard the phone ring, but he didn't answer it. Let the machine pick up, he thought, because he sure as hell didn't want to talk to anyone. Except Alex. And he'd fixed it so that she wouldn't be calling him.

The voice leaving the message didn't immediately register, but the words did. "Hey, old buddy, guess who this is? Answer the phone."

Luke rose, going to stand by the machine and listen. Old buddy? he wondered. The only person who'd ever called him that was James.

"I've got something of yours, old buddy," the familiar voice continued. "A nice tidy package. Built." He whistled admiringly. "Really built. Legs that go on forever. And long red hair . . ."

His stomach roiling, Luke snatched up the receiver. "You'd better be lying, James."

"You don't sound surprised to hear from me."

"I'm not. I figured it was you days ago."

"Bright, Luke. Very bright. But too late. Say hello, darlin'."

There was silence for a moment and then Luke heard something that sounded like flesh striking flesh. His hand tightened on the receiver. So James had seen Alex, knew what she looked like. That didn't prove that he had her—but his gut twisted at the idea.

"Shy, I guess," James said. "Don't worry, she'll talk in a minute. In the meantime, if you want to see her again, I've got some directions for you to follow. Number one, don't bring the cops. I've got a bomb with your lady's name on it. I'd hate to set it off without you, but a bunch of cops would make me real nervous. One's enough. Especially a redheaded lady cop. Yeah, she's something."

"Give it up, James. You don't have anyone with you."

"No? Guess I'll have to prove it to you."

Praying it was a bluff, Luke waited, trying to convince himself she was too smart for James to have gotten her. Alex was a cop. She wouldn't have let herself be jumped. She paid attention to things like that, he thought, remembering how she'd reacted in the parking lot when he'd approached her.

But she'd been upset when she left that night. More than upset, she'd been devastated. He doubted she'd been thinking about her personal safety.

"Come on, honey," James said. "Tell him you're here with me or I'll start the timer right now."

Luke heard her curse and his heart sank. "Alex? Alex, are you all right?"

"He's bluffing, Luke. He's just trying to get you here. Don't play into his hands. Call the police. Let them handle this. Don't you dare—"

"Alex, is there a bomb?"

Her brief hesitation only made him more certain there was. "It doesn't matter. Call the police. Do it—"

James's voice overrode hers. "Okay, listen up. Are you listening to me, Luke?"

"I'm listening, you son of a bitch."

James's laughter crackled over the airwaves. "Take LBJ Freeway to Highway Eighty, then you take the first Forney exit. You drive two-point-three miles and you're going to see a field on your right. There's a car in the middle of that field. You come now, you come alone, and you just might have a chance to save the lady here. Otherwise, you got no chance. Not even half a chance."

"Let her go. I'll come out there, but let her go. This is between you and me. Leave her out of it."

James laughed again. "Oh, I don't think so. I like her, even if she is a mouthy bitch."

"If you hurt her, you bastard, you're a dead man."

"Better hurry, old buddy. She's a real looker, which I don't have to tell you. No telling how I'm gonna pass the time until you get here."

The good news, Alex thought, was that other than drag her from the passenger seat to the driver's seat and handcuff her to the steering wheel, Bennett hadn't touched her again. After hearing his part of the conversation, she'd been afraid that his hatred of Luke would lead him to slapping her around some more at the least, or at the worst, raping her. Thank God she'd escaped that particular fate.

Unfortunately, his next move had been to plant a bomb on the dashboard of the car.

As far as she could tell, it was a simple time bomb, an improvised explosive device of a type she was very familiar with. With the proper equipment, she could have disarmed it fairly easily—if she hadn't been handcuffed to the steering wheel, booby-trapped to initiate the bomb if she was cut loose. At least, he hadn't set the timer yet. Obviously, he was waiting for Luke to arrive.

Bennett had left the driver's-side window rolled down, though she wasn't sure why. She assumed he wanted Luke to be able to see her, talk to her. A pleasant little form of torture, she thought.

She heard the whir of cicadas, an occasional dog barking, the faint sounds of desultory traffic from the highway several miles off. The moon played hide-and-seek with clouds, and stars twinkled intermittently in the dark sky. An ordinary night, an ordinary setting. But there was nothing ordinary about being trapped in a car with a bomb.

She couldn't call Bennett a madman. No, he was quite eerily . . . ordinary. Sane. And he intended to blow her up, and Luke along with her.

"What are you going to do if he doesn't come?" she finally asked him.

He was outside leaning against the car door, smoking a cigarette, the red tip glowing in the darkness. At her question he turned to look at her. "He'll come. I know Luke. He'll come."

"Why do you hate him so much?"

He took another drag of his cigarette, blew the smoke out slowly. "We used to be friends. Then we were like brothers. Brothers." He gave an angry laugh. "Some brother he turned out to be. Luke owed me. And instead of paying, he sold me out. So when fate played into my hands, I decided he would pay after all."

"Your cover is blown. The DA knows you're alive, knows that you were framing

Luke. He'll know who's responsible if either of us dies."

Illuminated by the moon coming out from behind a cloud, his grin flashed. "Too bad I'll be long gone by then." He flicked his cigarette down into the long grass and ground it out beneath his shoe. "Wouldn't want to start a fire. Yet," he added with a self-satisfied laugh. "Seems to me you should be worried about saving your own tail instead of Luke's."

"Why don't you cut your losses and just get out now? Why add murder to the list of crimes?"

Leaning down, he lost some of his smugness and snarled at her. "If you'd just done your job, it wouldn't have come to this. I mean, what about that bank deposit? Didn't you find it? All the evidence—"

"All the evidence was circumstantial. And yes, I knew about the deposit. Luke came to me with the information. That's when we started to believe he was being framed."

"I don't get it. What the hell made you believe him? After that clipping about his old man, I figured you'd haul him in for sure."

Something flickered behind him. She couldn't be sure, but her heart started to pound, her skin tingled. "What his father was has nothing to do with the man Luke is. Blood doesn't always make a difference." She looked him over with a sneer. "Obviously. Take you and your parents. From what I understand, they were decent people."

Her head jerked back from the force of his slapping her across the mouth. She tasted blood, felt her lip begin to swell immediately.

"You shut up about my parents. You don't know anything. All you know is some lies Luke's been feeding you."

James ought to be an expert on lies, Luke thought as he approached the car. He'd been living one for the last year. Was he making a mistake, trying to surprise James? Taking him on by himself? If this backfired . . . If it backfired he wouldn't be around to know it, but that was small consolation since Alex wouldn't be either.

He should have called the cops, or at least shouldn't have ditched his tail. But he'd been afraid to risk it. Not with Alex in James's hands. Not when he knew that if James even smelled the cops, he'd blow Alex away.

"Were you jealous?" he heard Alex ask. "That they took him in? You're jealous still, aren't you? All this isn't about Luke owing you, it's about you feeling inadequate. It's about you resenting him because of his success. Resenting him because your parents loved him."

Keep talking, Alex, Luke thought. That's it,

sweetheart. Just keep him occupied a couple more minutes, and I'll have the bastard.

"Shut up!" James yelled, and slugged her.

Luke launched himself at James just as the other man's fist connected with Alex's face. Cursing himself for not being quicker, Luke wrapped his arm around James's neck and tightened it as he dragged him backward. He was tempted, especially after seeing him hit Alex, to simply break his neck. He hadn't forgotten that part of his training.

He couldn't do it, though. Not like this. But he could sure as hell threaten him. "I can break your neck with one twist, James. Is that what you want?"

"You—wouldn't," James said, panting between the words.

"Don't count on it."

"Watch his hands!" Alex shouted. "He's going for a detonator."

Luke grabbed James's arms, managing to get one behind his back and jamming it high. James was quick, though, and he knew how Luke fought. He twisted away and they crashed to the ground and rolled, over and over, in a desperate bid for supremacy.

Dodging a knee to the groin, Luke emerged on top and felt a satisfying crunch of bone when his fist slammed into James's nose. Too soon to celebrate, though, because James's hands closed around his throat. Just before passing out, Luke managed to break his hold, but the next instant James rolled and pinned him beneath him.

Pain exploded in Luke's head as James's fist connected with his jaw. Dazed, he shook it off, jammed two fingers into James's carotid artery, and threw him over his head. Luke didn't give him a chance to do more than choke before he finished the job, delivering his best knockout punch, perfected when he was in the navy.

Panting, gulping in air greedily, Luke tried to think of something to immobilize James with. The best he could do was each of their belts. One belt took care of the legs, the other he used to secure James's hands behind his back. He emptied the other man's pockets for good measure, making sure to place the detonator out of James's reach.

Shakily, he rose and looked at the car. He could just make her out in the moonlight—a slash of red hair and a very white face in the open window.

Reaching the car, he leaned down into the window, took her face in trembling hands, and kissed her. When he thought how close he'd come to losing her . . .

"Thank God you're all right." He drew back and looked at her, searching her face. "You are all right, aren't you? He didn't—"

"No, I'm okay."

Her voice was husky, and the sound of it

was the most beautiful thing he'd ever heard in his life. He kissed her again, rough and desperate, and then reached out to open her door.

"Luke, wait. Listen."

"Listen to what? I don't hear any . . ." His voice trailed off as they stared at each other, straining to hear in the silence.

The clock ticked.

FIFTEEN

"Son of a bitch," Luke said, his gaze still locked with hers. "He activated the timer."

"Sounds like it." Her throat was so dry, Alex could hardly speak, but she forced the words out. "And I'm—" Her breath hitched and she had to start over. "I'm handcuffed to the steering wheel."

Even the dim moonlight couldn't hide the shock in his eyes. "If I get you out of those handcuffs—"

"You can't. He set it up so that cutting me loose would initiate the bomb."

Luke let out a long, vicious string of curses. "I should have killed him when I had the chance. How much time?"

"About fifteen minutes, I think. The interior light was on while he set everything up, and I got a look at the timer."

"Fifteen minutes," Luke repeated. "Why so long?"

"The better to torture you."

"Yeah, that's been his plan all along. The bomb's in there with you?"

Biting her lip, she nodded. "Attached to the dash."

"Easier access than underneath the car, at least. You're going to have to tell me how to disarm it."

"No. It's too risky." She didn't give a damn what he said, she wasn't willing to risk his life. "Call for help."

"No time."

"Dammit, Luke, call for backup!"

"Screw backup. We're out here in the middle of East Nowhere. There's no time for them to get here and you know it."

She did know it. But she also knew how dangerous it was for him to even be near her, much less to defuse a bomb.

"Alex." He put his hand on her shoulder and squeezed hard. "We've got fifteen—less than fifteen—damn minutes. We don't have time to argue. I brought some tools with me from my car in case we got the chance to use them. A flashlight"—he held it up to show her—"a needle-nose pliers, and a wire cutter. You have to tell me how to disarm that bomb."

"Luke, no. If it doesn't work, you'll die."

"And if we don't try it, you'll die. Accept it, Alex. I'm not leaving you."

She stared at him, at the determined set of his jaw, the fierce look in his eyes. Hadn't she known that would be his response? Should she waste precious time arguing or do as he said and accept the fact that he would stay no matter what she said?

"I shouldn't let you risk it."

"Neither of us has a choice. Do you really imagine I'm going to leave you here without trying to save you?"

No, she didn't imagine that. Choices. Instincts. Hunches. She didn't like the odds. But it was pointless, and dangerous, to argue further. She closed her eyes, then opened them to look at him.

"It's a time pencil," she finally said. "Are you familiar with those?"

"I remember seeing one or two of them. I'm not familiar enough with them to do much good, though."

"We need a pin. Either a straight pin or a ballpoint pen. Do you have something like that?"

He patted his pockets. "Nothing other than what I just told you."

"All right. Do you see my purse anywhere? He must have brought it because these are my handcuffs."

He played the flashlight over the interior of

the car. "On the floorboard on the passenger side."

"Good. My police badge is in my purse. It has a pin on it. But . . ." She hesitated before adding, "You're going to have to get in the car to get it."

Their gazes met and held for an endless moment. He would know, she realized, exactly what—and who—she was thinking about. Jenna. Was she to share Jenna's fate after all? And Luke as well?

"Don't," he said sharply. "Don't remember the past. This is right now, and it has nothing to do with what happened before. We can do this, Alex."

"I—oh, God, I can't think."

"Yes you can. It's what you're trained for." His hand tightened on her shoulder, giving her strength, giving her courage. "Steady. Take a minute, and then tell me which door. You can do it. I know you can do it."

Door number one or door number two, she thought, with the stakes life or death. She tried to review the facts as she would have with any other case. If not for the voice that kept whispering that if she screwed up, she would kill not only herself but Luke, too, she might have succeeded.

She choked down on her fear long enough to consider the options. Her instincts and her training told her that no matter how professionally the original job had been executed, James Bennett wasn't a pro. And that knowledge told her which door to choose. It hadn't worked for Jenna, but that had been a case involving someone who knew how a bomb squad worked. Who knew the training drill. With any luck at all, James wouldn't.

"The right rear door," she said, then whispered, "Kiss me in case I'm wrong."

He smiled, squeezed her shoulder again, and shook his head. "Trust your instincts. I do."

It couldn't have taken him longer than ten seconds to round the rear of the car, yet each second stretched like time in a warp. Her nerves, wound tight to begin with, coiled to the breaking point. She wanted to scream, to cry, to curse, to pray. And she did all of those things during those few mind-numbing seconds.

She was afraid to look. She was afraid not to. When she turned her head, the darkness was complete and she could see nothing. Her heart was laboring like a racehorse running the Kentucky Derby, pounding so hard she could barely breathe. The door handle made a squeaky sound as he pulled it up. Her mind sang out an incoherent prayer as Luke opened the door.

Seconds later she felt him crawling over the seat and then he was beside her, kissing her fiercely, desperately, and she was laughing and crying and kissing him back, every bit as frantic as he. She wanted to touch him, hold him . . . and then she remembered why that was impossible.

He drew back and stroked a finger down her cheek. "What did I say? Piece of cake."

She gave a shaky, slightly hysterical laugh. "Let's just hope the rest goes as smoothly as that did. What did you do to Bennett?"

Holding the flashlight in one hand, he dug in her purse. "I didn't kill him. But if I'd realized he had you hooked to the steering wheel, I would have. I tied him up with our belts, in case he came to and decided to cause us some more trouble. Or tried to run."

A few seconds later he found the badge and jerked the pin out of it. Holding it up to show her, he said, "Got it. What now?"

"Get my keys out so you can unlock my handcuffs." If they got that far, she thought, but she didn't think it necessary to add that. "Give me the flashlight," she continued. "I think I can aim it at the bomb so you can work. I'm afraid turning on the interior lights would trip something."

He arranged the flashlight in her hands, then leaned forward to study the bomb himself.

"Do you see the inspection holes?" she asked him. "There, along the top of that tube that's sticking up."

"Yeah, I see them."

"You're going to stick that pin through them, without touching the bomb or the time pencil itself. Got that? Don't touch anything, just slide the pin through the holes. That will deactivate the timer."

He turned his head to look at her. "And if I do touch something?"

She smiled in spite of everything. "Well, the good news is I doubt we'll know it."

The few seconds that it took him to slide the pin in seemed to last aeons. She held her breath and waited, wondering how he could seem so calm when there was so much at stake.

"Okay," he said a moment later. With a cocky smile, he added, "Guess I didn't touch anything."

Relief rushed through her, but it wasn't over yet. "Is the timer still running?"

He looked back at the dash. "No. The clock is stopped. Is that it, then?"

"Now you have to make sure the cuffs are disconnected from the bomb. Is there a wire leading to the timer or the bomb itself?"

"To the timer. But since it's deactivated—"

She shook her head. "Doesn't matter. Cut the wire."

For a moment he simply stared at her. "But won't that . . . Couldn't that initiate the bomb?"

"Yes. But so could anything else we do.

This type of explosive device is unstable at the best of times. By deactivating the timer, we've put even more stress on it. It can still blow at any moment. Anything can inititate it. Even something like a cellular phone being used nearby. Or opening the wrong door of the car."

He let out a long breath. "Okay, you've convinced me. We cut it."

She watched as he opened the wire cutters over the trip wire. "Wait!"

Pausing, he turned his head to look at her.

"I love you, Luke. I wanted you to know that in case anything . . ." Unable to complete the sentence, she let her voice trail off.

He leaned over and kissed her. "For luck," he said, and closed the wire cutters.

It took them both a second to realize there had been no explosion and they were still alive. Luke fumbled with the lock of her handcuffs and then she was free. She jerked her hands out of the cuffs and cried, "The window! Don't open the doors! Go out the window!" His hands were at her waist, boosting her up and then, on her rump, shoving her out the open window.

Alex hit the ground and rolled. She heard Luke drop down heavily beside her and felt relief flood through her.

Then they were stumbling, running, trying to get as far away from the car as possible.

Luke's hand was at her back, urging her on, pushing her faster. Gasping for breath, she was grateful for the help. Finally, they halted and she fell to the ground, her head bowed, sucking in desperate gulps of air. It was a long moment before she realized Luke was no longer beside her. She raised her head and saw him running back toward the car.

Oh, my God, she thought in blank shock. He's gone back for Bennett.

Why hadn't he left him? Even as she watched in dawning horror she knew that Luke would no more have left Bennett than he'd have left her. She saw him drop down beside the prone form, and then, a few seconds later, they were both up and running. Ten feet, twenty, fifty. The distance between the two men and the car lengthened, and time slogged on as if caught in quicksand.

Alex rose and started toward them.

A siren shrieked in the still of the night. Seconds later, she heard a roaring boom and the night exploded around her. The ground shook like an earthquake beneath her feet, and as she fell, knocked flat by the blast, she saw the car go up in flames. Red, orange, yellow streams of flame leaped upward and smoke billowed, inky black against the dark sky.

Struggling to her feet, she started running to Luke again. She found him lying facedown with Bennett a few yards behind him. Adrenaline surged through her with a screaming rush as she rolled him over, hooked her hands beneath his arms, and pulled him backward. She needed all her strength, and some she hadn't known she possessed, to drag him.

By the time the second explosion occurred, she'd gone as far as she could go. Collapsing beside him, she felt frantically for his pulse. Tears poured down her face when she felt it beating steadily beneath her fingers.

His hand came up and covered her shaking one. "Either it's raining or you're crying," he said huskily.

"You idiot!" If she hadn't been so glad he was alive, she'd have killed him for scaring her so badly. She pulled his head onto her lap and touched his face, his chest, laid her palm over his heart. "You should have left him. He wasn't worth going back for."

"Old habits . . . die hard. Where is he?"

She glanced back to where she'd last seen him, but all she saw was burning grass. "Dead, I think. He got caught in the second blast. The gas tank exploded."

"You saved my life."

"Considering you had saved mine earlier, it seemed like the thing to do."

The wail of sirens grew louder, sounding like more had been added to the first. Someone must have called the explosion in, Alex thought.

"Can you walk?" she asked Luke.

"If I have to. Why?"

"I'm afraid that fire is going to get here before the fire truck does. I'd like to get to the road."

Not surprisingly, he seemed a little shaky on his feet. Alex put her arm around his waist and started walking with him, away from the spreading flames.

"Before the cops and the firemen get here," he said after they'd walked awhile, "there's something I want to ask you."

"Save your strength. We can talk later."

"No, it's important."

She sighed. "All right. What is it?"

"Will you marry me?"

Her mouth fell open and she halted to stare at him. After the things he'd said to her earlier that night—had it just been that night?—she'd never imagined she'd hear those words from him. "Marry you? But you said—I thought you hated me because—"

"No." He shook his head, framing her face in his hands and smiling at her. "I didn't understand what you were doing. I felt betrayed, and I wanted to hate you. But I couldn't. I could never hate you."

He kissed her, a gentle brush of his lips over hers, and then continued. "When you searched my office and then arrested me . . ."

He hesitated, as if he wasn't quite sure what to say. "God, I don't ever want to hurt like that again. And you were so cold, so damned unfeeling. It felt like a dream. More of a nightmare."

She was clutching the front of his shirt, looking up at him. "I didn't think I could get through it if I didn't treat you impersonally. I kept telling myself it was just a job, but it was killing me, Luke."

"I thought you didn't believe me, that you'd never believed me. I thought you'd just been sleeping with me to help your case. Do you know what that did to me, Alex?"

"Yes," she whispered. "I couldn't tell you, though," she added helplessly.

"I know." He covered her hands with his and squeezed. "But at the time . . . at the time I didn't understand any of that. All I knew was that you'd destroyed me."

"I'm so sorry. I should have tried to—I should have reassured you, but I didn't know how. Not without compromising my investigation."

"Alex, I'm not telling you all this to make you feel worse. I'm trying to clear things between us. After you came to see me tonight, I started thinking, really thinking about what you'd said. And what you'd done. I couldn't bring myself to believe that everything we'd shared, everything we'd been to each other, had been an act on your part."

Her throat clogged with emotion. "Do you understand now why I had to arrest you? And that I'd have done anything not to have had to?"

"I finally figured out it was the only way you saw to get James to come into the open."

"It was. I knew you'd hate me, but I didn't have a choice. It wasn't just my job, Luke. I had to do something if I was going to clear you."

"I know that now, but I couldn't see it then. And when James called . . . God, I'd thought I couldn't feel worse than I did the day you arrested me, but that was nothing compared to how I felt when James told me he had you. I've never been so damned afraid in my life. I knew then that nothing that had happened, nothing you'd done mattered, as long as I could just find you safe. If he'd hurt you, killed you—"

He broke off and pulled her against him, burying his face in her hair while she murmured soothing words and held on tight.

He raised his head and looked down at her. "You haven't answered my question," he said, his mouth tilting in the smile she loved.

"You haven't said why you want to marry me."

"I love you, Alex. I fell in love with you the night we met."

"That's all it took for me too. Just one night."

"What do you say to a lifetime?"

"That sounds even better," she said, and kissed him.

EPILOGUE

Five months later

"Some reception," Waylon said to Luke, waving with his champagne glass to encompass the lobby of the newly opened Alsobrook building.

Luke nodded agreement. The interior designer Alsobrook had hired had done a nice job fitting the furnishings to the overall effect of spaciousness and elegance that Luke had striven to project in the structure of the building. Apparently, others had liked it as well. He had several new projects lined up, most of them a direct result of his work on this particular building.

Life was better than he'd ever imagined it could be. Especially since he had Alex to share it with now.

"Never saw so many pretty women in my

life," Waylon was saying. "And speaking of lookers . . ."

Luke turned to see Alex walking toward them. He smiled, glad she'd made it. Almost five months of marriage hadn't dulled the pleasure he got just from seeing her. "I was afraid you'd gotten held up at work," he told her, putting one arm around her in an unconsciously possessive gesture.

"I did, but not at work." She planted a lingering kiss on his mouth and then whispered in his ear, "I had to take a pregnancy test."

Before Luke could respond, she'd turned and was talking to Waylon. "Wait a minute." He gathered his wits. "You did what?"

"You heard me." Her mouth curved, her eyes sparkling mischievously.

"Waylon, excuse me while I talk to my wife." And throttle her for dropping that little bombshell and then leaving him hanging.

"Oh, you won't bother me. Go right ahead," Waylon said, grinning.

Ignoring him, Luke pinned Alex with a sharp gaze. "Well? Are you going to tell me? Yes or no?"

She lifted her chin and smiled at him. "Yes."

Stunned, he simply stared at her. A baby. Alex was having a baby. His baby. They'd talked about it, but had decided to wait. Fate, apparently, had other ideas.

"Shock," Alex said. "I'd say he was in shock. What do you say, Waylon?"

"Looks downright thunderstruck," Waylon agreed. "What did you say to him?"

"Just told him that one of his projects is going to come in ahead of schedule."

Luke finally regained command of his faculties and pulled her into his arms. Looking down into her eyes, he could see happiness, and a little apprehension. "You're sure?"

She nodded. "Positive."

He smiled. "I think this calls for a celebration. A private celebration. You and me. Later," he murmured against her lips.

"A new project, huh? What kind?" Waylon asked.

"We don't know yet," Alex said. "Ask us again in about seven months."

"You don't know?" Waylon repeated. "What kind of a project . . ." His voice trailed off and he stared at them while the knowledge dawned. "You two are having a kid?"

"That's what she tells me."

"Hey, congratulations!"

"Thanks. Do me a favor, Waylon. Get lost for a while."

Waylon grinned. "Want to be alone, huh? I can take a hint," he said, and left them.

"I know we were planning to wait," Alex said. "Do you mind?"

"Do I look like I mind?"

She considered him a moment. "No, you look happy. And smug."

"I feel smug. And happy. Seven months," he mused, linking hands with her and strolling toward the bank of elevators. "That would mean you got pregnant in San Diego. When we went to the Hotel Del Coronado for that long weekend a couple of months back."

Her mouth curved in a saucy smile. "That would make it about right. Funny what happens when we go to that place. So, are you going to show me around?"

"Absolutely. I know a private place that needs to be inspected for explosives."

She arched an eyebrow at him. "Bombs?"

"Not exactly." He gave her a wicked smile. "Let me show you. . . ."

THE EDITORS' CORNER

What do you get when you pit the forces of nature against the forces of man? You'll have a chance to find out after reading the four fantastic LOVE-SWEPTs coming your way next month. Two couples face the evil forces in their fellow man while the other two do battle with nature in the form of a snowstorm and a hurricane. The result is four mind-blowing romances that'll leaving you cheering—or crying—at the end!

Loveswept favorite Charlotte Hughes dazzles us with **JUST MARRIED . . . AGAIN**, LOVE-SWEPT #902. Ordered by the family doctor to take time off, Michael Kelly decides to spend Thanksgiving in his mountain cabin, away from the pressures of work. Maddie Kelly wants to spend the holiday in *her* mountain cabin, away from her well-meaning family and friends. Unfortunately, it's the same cabin. Since their separation nearly a year earlier, Maddie and Michael have been avoiding each other. When a sudden case of amnesia and a snowstorm trap them in the mountains, together with two dogs and a stowaway nephew, the couple have no choice but to endure each other's company. As they get to know each other and the unhappy people they've become, they slowly realize that what tore them apart the first time around could be the very thing that binds them together. Charlotte is at her all-time best in this touching novel of love rediscovered.

In the land of **SMOKE AND MIRRORS**, Laura Taylor paves the way for two lost souls in LOVE-SWEPT #903. Anxious to begin a new life, Bailey Kincaid fled from Hollyweird with divorce papers in hand. As co-owner and president of Kincaid Drilling, she's responsible for the safety of her men, and she's determined to make the person who is sabotaging her job site pay. When Patrick Sutton found himself interested in the shy wife of one of his clients, he immediately distanced himself from her. He's stunned to find out the woman who captured his attention years ago is now the strong-willed woman in charge of the construction on his property. Patrick had taught her how it felt to ache for something she could never have, and it hadn't been easy to get him out of her system. He insists that they were never strangers and that they deserve to follow where their hearts seem determined to lead. But can the sorrow that haunted their nights finally be put to rest? Laura Taylor writes a memorable story of fated lovers who discover the great gift of second chances.

In **ONLY YESTERDAY**, LOVESWEPT #904, Peggy Webb teases us with a timeless romance that knows no bounds. A sense of *knowing*, a sense of belonging, and a sense of love have kept Ann Debeau in Fairhope, Alabama. When she haggles with Colt Butler over a charming clock, she's pleasantly surprised at the attraction she feels for the handsome stranger. Sorting through her grandmother's belongings in the attic, Ann Debeau finds a stack of love letters addressed to a man she's never heard of. A hurricane strands her there with the waters swirling ever higher, and Colt comes to her rescue, only to be stuck right alongside her. As they read the letters, a mysterious force whisks them in time to a place where both have been before and into a relationship that was never consummated. In the past, Colt and Ann find a ghost that demands closure and an enduring love that refuses to give up on forever. Peggy Webb challenges us to believe in destiny and reincarnation, in this jewel of a Loveswept.

And in **LOVING LINDSEY,** LOVESWEPT #905, Pat Van Wie introduces neighboring ranchers and one-time best friends Lindsey Baker and Will Claxton. Years ago, a misunderstanding drove Will from Willowbend, Wyoming, but he's always known that one day he would return to the land he loves best. Never one to desert a lady in need, he offers Lindsey help in sorting out the trouble at her ranch. Though he swears he's looking to buy his land back from her fair and square, Lindsey's sure that Will is the one responsible for the "accidents." When one night of promises in the moonlight leads to more than just kisses, the dueling ranchers realize they're not just fighting for her land. In the end, will the face of her betrayer belong to the man she's dreamed of for so long . . . or the man she's trusted for all of her life? Pat Van Wie proves once more that those we love first are so often those we love forever.

Happy reading!

With warmest wishes,

Susann Brailey *Joy Abella*

Susann Brailey   Joy Abella
Senior Editor   Administrative Editor